IN THE DEPTHS OF THE ENDLESS CATACOMBS!

Your party has journeyed deep into the dreaded Endless Catacombs in an attempt to put a stop to the curse that plagues the land.

You know that the source of the curse is very near now, somewhere beyond the mysterious door just ahead. As you pass through the door, a powerful voice booms, "I am the Guardian! Who goes there?"

Trembling, you look up to face the most fearsome creature you ever saw—an iron golem! Drawing its huge, gleaming sword, the metallic monster begins to advance straight toward you!

What will you do?

1) If you think your party should attempt to fight the golem, turn to page 96.

2) If you want your wizard companion to try to use a magic spell on the creature, turn to page 136.

3) If you decide to leave the room and return the way you came, turn to page 65.

Whatever your decision is, you are certain to find danger lurking around every bend in
THE ENDLESS CATACOMBS

THE ENDLESS CATACOMBS

BY MARGARET BALDWIN WEIS

A DUNGEONS & DRAGONS™ ADVENTURE BOOK

Cover and Interior Art by Jeff Easley

TSR, Inc.

To Janet and Gary Pack,
fellow dungeoners, and to John Lehman,
our dungeon master

THE ENDLESS CATACOMBS
© Copyright 1984, TSR, Inc.
All Rights Reserved.

Distributed to the book trade in the United States by Random House, Inc., and in Canada by Random House of Canada, Ltd.

Distributed in the United Kingdom by TSR (UK), Ltd. Distributed to the toy and hobby trade by regional distributors.

DUNGEONS & DRAGONS and PICK A PATH TO ADVENTURE are trademarks owned by TSR, Inc.

D&D and ENDLESS QUEST are registered trademarks owned by TSR, Inc.

First printing: September, 1984
Printed in the United States of America
Library of Congress Catalog Card Number: 84-51001
ISBN: 0-88038-162-0

9 8 7 6 5 4 3 2 1

TSR, Inc.
P.O. Box 756
Lake Geneva, WI 53147

TSR (UK), Ltd.
The Mill, Rathmore Road
Cambridge CB1 4AD
United Kingdom

Ou are about to set off on an adventure in which YOU will meet many dangers — and face many decisions. YOUR choices will determine how the story turns out. So be careful . . . you must choose wisely!

Do not read this book from beginning to end! Instead, as you are faced with a decision, follow the instructions and keep turning to the pages where your choices lead you until you come to an end. At any point, YOUR choice could bring success — or disaster!

You can read THE ENDLESS CATACOMBS many times, with many different results, so if you make an unwise choice, go back to the beginning and start again!

Good luck on YOUR adventure!

In this story, you are Gregor, a young orphan who has been raised by gypsies since you were three. Although they have always been kind enough to you, now that you are approaching manhood, you are expected to earn your keep—as a thief. As the story begins, you stand outside the gates of a city plagued by a mysterious curse, and you face a dilemma. . . .

"Get going, boy." Hugo shoves you roughly from behind with his hand. "They'll be opening the gates in a few minutes. Jump into the crowd when the peasants move forward and make your way through with them."

You stumble ahead reluctantly, feeling Hugo's rough hand pushing you every few steps.

"It doesn't seem worth the effort," you mutter, stalling.

"Aye. You're right there, boy." Hugo scratches his bearded chin. "This village is a place of evil . . . cursed. We'll find slim pickings here, I'm afraid."

Hugo pulls a sparkling piece of crystal from his belt and rubs it three times. Then he slips it back into a pocket.

"It's a good thing I have my lucky crystal," he mutters, "or I wouldn't set foot in this accursed town." He shrugs in futility. "But then, times are hard all over. Perhaps the curse is spreading, like the old woman says. Anyway, we must eat. We'll split up now. Meet me inside the gates."

You watch in disgust as Hugo pushes through the crowd of peasants waiting at the city gates for the market to open. Familiar with the tricks of his trade, you see the thief bump into a peddler, apologize, then walk away, stuffing the man's purse into his shirt.

Sickened, you move to the edge of the crowd and lean up against a wall, staring down at your boots.

People glance at you suspiciously as they pass. You don't much blame them. You are dressed in a gaudy, multicolored silk shirt with long, flowing sleeves. A wide sash encircles your waist. Your gaily striped pants are tucked into worn leather boots. You fit right into the gypsy camp where you live, but you seem out of place among the shabbily dressed peasants in this forsaken town.

You know that Hugo will expect you to have something to show for your morning's work when he meets you inside the gates. He's sure to be angry if you turn up empty-handed. You run your hand along your jaw ruefully, already feeling his heavy fist with its gold rings knocking you into the dust.

Although the gypsies who raised you have been kind enough to you, they have little patience with a boy your age who cannot contribute to the welfare of the wandering band.

"He has the makings of a good thief," you overheard Hugo tell the old woman only a few days ago. "He's quick and agile, and his hands are slender and skilled."

But something dies in you at the thought of stealing. The old woman understands this.

"Remember," she told Hugo, "he was not born a gypsy. His mother, rest her soul, was a lady of high birth."

"Bah! He can earn his keep like the rest of us!" Hugo snarled.

"Let him read the tarot cards. He has a talent for that," the old woman pleaded.

"Woman's talent!" Hugo grumbled. "Let him earn his keep like a man!"

And so you stand outside the gates of this wretched city, known to be under a terrible curse, supposedly on your first thieving raid.

Suddenly you hear a horn blow. The city gates swing open, and the crowd surges forward, carrying you along. You find yourself caught up in a mob of peasants, squealing pigs, bleating sheep, and barking dogs. Carts and wagons rumble past. You allow the crowd to carry you into the marketplace. You look around, wondering what to do next, when suddenly a hand grabs hold of your shirt and drags you off into a dark, filthy alley.

"Well, what have you got?" Hugo's dark eyes leer down at you expectantly.

You hesitate. Hugo's free hand closes into a fist.

"Come, Gregor. The old woman isn't around this time to stop me from giving you the beating you deserve!"

You gulp. Perhaps you can make up some sort of a story and escape the beating. On the other hand, you could tell Hugo exactly what you think of stealing.

1) If you decide to try to make up a story to avoid being beaten by Hugo, turn to page 66.

2) But if you decide to stand up to Hugo and tell him the truth, turn to page 94.

"This way!" The wizard turns abruptly and heads for the north door, moving faster than you've ever seen him go. His robes whip around his ankles and his staff thumps the ground.

You hesitate, looking back at your companions. None of them says a word, but you seem to feel their thoughts tugging at you. Then you look at Luben Warlock, and your throat closes with fear. A meteor swarm sounds too awful to face! You can imagine the terrible flame and the roar as the four meteors flare out from the magician's fingers.

"I'm sorry," you shout and run off after the wizard. Your brother follows, a look of relief on his face.

You dash through the north door, your brother close behind you, and hurry through the tomb. All of a sudden, the blue light vanishes, and you are plunged into darkness so thick you seem to be smothering in it.

"Brother!" you shout, reaching for his hand.

He grabs your hand and gasps, "Where's the wizard?"

"I don't know!" you say fearfully.

Suddenly the corridor is lighted by a brilliant orange glow from the room you left behind. You hear the sound of a violent explosion, and then everything is dark and quiet once more.

You and your brother stare into the darkness, trembling. "Eric?" you quaver. "Father Justin?" There is no answer.

"Surely they're dead," your brother says.

"Then Luben will be after us now," you whisper.

"We're all alone in the darkness," your brother murmurs softly. "What chance do we have?"

The two of you stand side by side. You have no torches, no weapons. Too late, you realize your mistake.

"Don't worry," Lord Bloodstone says after a moment. "We'll find our way out."

"Yeah," you gulp, glad he can't see your face.

For you and your newfound brother, the adventure has come to an . . .

END

"The air smells better down this way," you declare, pointing to the south door. "And I don't hear any wererats."

"Right!" Eric agrees. "Let's go south."

You follow Eric down a twisting corridor, with Grimpen's staff lighting the way. The walls are dry and clean, and there is no evidence of wererats in this passage. The air begins to smell more and more fragrant as the sound of wererats fades behind you.

"I wonder why the wererats don't come down here," Father Justin says.

"Maybe they don't like places that smell better than they do," you chuckle.

The corridor widens. His sword drawn, Eric walks beside the wizard. There is no sign of danger.

The wizard's staff suddenly lights a small room you have entered.

"Dead end," Eric says with a frown and moves to guard the entrance leading back south.

"The wine cellar," Grimpen notes with satisfaction, shining his light on racks of old bottles covered with dust. "Rare vintages from all over the world were brought for our enjoyment during the wizards' conclave."

Lord Bloodstone's eyes glitter in anticipation in the light of the wizard's staff. Eagerly he walks over to the bottles.

"I wouldn't drink any of that!" Father Justin warns. "You don't need any wine to keep your courage up, my lord."

"We need you sober," Eric adds grimly.

"Just one drink." Bloodstone picks up a bottle in trembling hands. "Here's a rare vintage from the elvish lands! I've heard it gives any traveler the strength to keep going for miles without rest. What do you say?" He turns to you. "Will you sample the wine with me, Gregor?"

"Is it really elvish wine?" Father Justin asks, stepping forward to peer at the bottle.

"Don't touch it!" Eric warns. "Remember what Seventhson told us. It may be a trap!"

"But if it is elvish wine," Father Justin argues, "the strength it will provide could be a help on our quest."

"What do you say, wizard?" Lord Bloodstone asks.

"I say you are all a pack of fools!" Grimpen sniffs. "You may drink elvish wine all day and night if you have a mind to."

"Well, Gregor? Will you join me?" Lord Bloodstone asks once more, uncorking the bottle.

1) Remembering that the wererats won't even come into this room, you side with Eric and refuse. If this is your choice, turn to page 73.

2) If Father Justin thinks it might be all right, you decide one little sip can't harm you. If you want to sample the wine, turn to page 78.

"Father Justin's right, Eric," you plead. "You can count on me—and on my brother," you add hesitantly, looking at Lord Bloodstone.

"It's been years since I've had faith in anything but a bottle," Bloodstone says slowly. "But perhaps I can find faith in something else down there. . . . I will do my best, Eric. That is all I can promise."

"You'd better hope the success of the quest doesn't depend on me," the wizard sneers. "The only reason I'm going is to find an ancient spellbook my master left down there. I care nothing for your cause."

"Can't we leave him behind?" you hear Eric whisper to Father Justin. "Couldn't you put a Hold Spell on him?"

"Not on such a powerful magic-user," Father Justin replies, shaking his head. "Stop and think, Eric. We've all been brought here for a purpose. Seventhson was allowed to live, while none of the others survived. There must be some good in him. . . ."

Lord Bloodstone grabs a torch from a sconce on the wall and leads the way down the stairs. You follow your brother, swallowing hard as you duck through the low doorway. Grimpen Seventhson comes behind you, his wizard's staff clutched in one hand. Eric follows, carrying another torch.

The narrow stairway winds down in a steep spiral. Lord Bloodstone slips, and you take the torch from his shaking grip.

You come to the end of the stairs. Ahead of you is a wide room, with small niches in the wall. At the far end, an archway is blocked up with bricks. It seems to be a hasty job. The bricks are piled every which way. Gobs of mortar litter the floor.

"The workmen fled before they finished," Bloodstone says. "I finished the job myself."

"Still, it looks strong," Eric comments. "It could take us days to knock it down."

"Days!" you cry in alarm.

"Oh, stand aside," Grimpen orders in disgust. The wizard looks into a pouch hanging from his belt. Frowning, he peers into another. Finally he reaches into the second pouch and removes something. Standing before the wall, he raises one hand and recites a long string of words. With his other hand, he throws some small seeds on the floor.

As you watch in amazement, an opening begins to appear in the wall. Soon the hole is high enough to step through. Not knowing what to expect, you start through the arch.

As you do so, fear grows within you until you begin to shake violently. With a cry, you fall to the ground. "I—I can't go in there!" you cry.

"Nor I," Lord Bloodstone says, sagging against a wall, his face gray.

"You must do something, Father," Eric urges, his voice trembling. "I have faced every manner of evil in this world, yet I can't go in there without help! There is a Fear Spell blocking us!"

"Yes, of course." Father Justin lays his hand on your head, murmuring soft words. Immediately the terrible fear vanishes, leaving you feeling peaceful and calm. The cleric touches each of the others and all begin to breathe easier—except the wizard.

"Keep your hands off of me, cleric!" Grimpen growls. "I need none of your spells."

Father Justin shrugs.

The company advances swiftly now. You walk into a narrow passageway. Holding the torch high, you glance around. The passageway is littered with bones and other remains of animals. The stench is sickening. Here and there lie a battered shield or a broken knife.

"What is all this?" you ask, wrinkling your nose.

"Wererats!" Eric exclaims grimly. "They've been here recently, too, from the smell of things."

"Ah," Father Justin says, pointing. Before you, the passageway comes to an end, and you see a wall with a dark doorway.

"The Room of the Four Winds," Grimpen Seventhson whispers.

"Why do they call it that?" you ask.

"You'll see," the wizard says shortly.

"Enter cautiously," Eric warns, drawing his sword.

Please turn to page 22.

"Gregor! What have you done?" Father Justin cries. He hurries over to the aged wizard, who is lying on the floor, unconscious.

"I couldn't let him get that book of black magic," you say, beginning to feel ashamed. "I didn't mean to hit him that hard."

"You had to do it, Gregor!" Eric says grimly.

"No, he didn't." The Blue Lady rushes into the room and hurriedly studies the book. "This is the great Ian Whitestone's spellbook! Grimpen could have used this to help us get past the golem!"

"But now he'll never have the chance!" laughs an evil voice.

"Luben Warlock!" You look around but see nothing.

"Thank you for this wonderful gift, gypsy. At last my enemy is in my power! And you will be next, Blue Lady, once I have taken the old wizard with me. I will return shortly. . . ."

You hear the evil laughter, and Grimpen's body begins to glow red, then start to fade.

"Quick! Out the south door!" Eric shouts.

But it is too late. You stare in horror as iron bars crash down all around you, blocking every door—except the door to the north.

And as you listen, you hear the sound of something heavy moving toward you. The golem has left its post and is approaching. . . .

You realize you can fight the golem or fight Luben. Unfortunately, both choices lead to . . .

THE END

Quickly you lunge for the knife. "At least I'll die in a fair fight," you think grimly. You know that Hugo is especially skilled at knife-fighting, a popular form of recreation in the gypsy camp. His grin splits his black beard as you rise to face him, the knife cradled loosely in your hand. Stealing a glance at your knife, you notice that the dagger has a snake's head and strange runes delicately carved on the thin blade.

Instantly a noisy crowd gathers, glad for a chance to forget their own problems. The cleric looks on in silence, though you hear him chanting softly.

"Give up, Gregor!" Hugo snarls. "Drop the knife and take your thrashing like a man!"

"You'll never turn me into a thief!" you yell. "I'd rather die."

"So be it," Hugo mutters.

Slowly you and Hugo circle each other, watching for an opening. You know you're no match for the skilled gypsy. All you can do is try to defend yourself and trust to luck.

Hugo slashes at you. Desperately you parry his attack, then feel a fiery sensation spreading through your arm. Suddenly you feel the knife hilt seem to slither in your grasp. Startled, you almost drop it.

In your hand, you feel the snake-knife come alive. Guiding your arm, it begins to fight on its own, flashing in the sunlight. You find yourself stabbing and slashing with unbelievable skill.

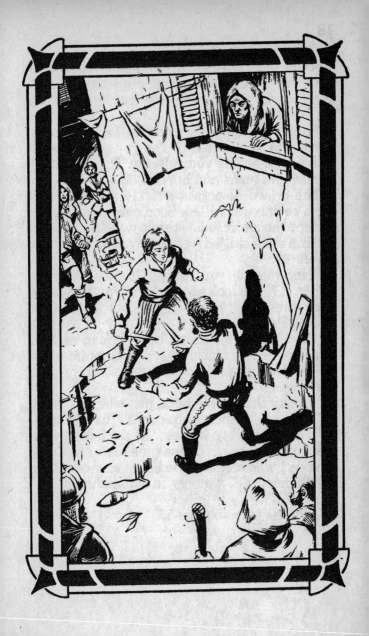

Hugo backs away in confusion, his eyes growing wild. Suddenly he slips and falls to the ground. Seizing the opportunity, you leap on top of him.

"Hold!" Hugo cries, and you feel the knife grow cold in your hand. The gypsy scrambles to his feet, eyeing you sullenly. Then, without a word, he turns and hurries off.

The crowd disperses quickly, disappointed that no one was killed. Soon everyone is gone except the cleric, who stands watching you.

"You are a skilled fighter, my son," the cleric observes.

"Not really," you reply. "It's this strange knife...." You look at the cleric, remembering that the knife was lying at his feet. "Is it yours, Father?"

"No!" the cleric says slowly. "I can neither touch nor carry sharp objects. The knife is not mine—though perhaps I know something of its origin."

"Lucky that it was here, just when I needed it," you say, glancing sharply at the cleric.

"I do not believe in luck," he says, returning your gaze evenly. "It was meant to be here, just as I was meant to be here—to meet you."

"To meet me!" you cry in astonishment.

Please turn to page 55.

"Wererats!" you cry out. "Coming at us from two directions. I'm getting out of here!"

Terrible childhood memories flood your mind. Running in panic, you dash back through the north door. A chill wind greets you as you enter the door.

Behind you, the cleric calls out something. Then Eric shouts, and you hear the clang of sword against shield. The wererats are attacking! You dash through the hole the wizard made in the brick wall, then stop.

What made you run like that? Ashamed, you stare down the passageway. The sound of fighting fades, and you hear Father Justin's voice calling you. Taking a deep breath, you start back through the arch. Then the terrible fear assails you—the Fear Spell!

Quaking, you fall back. "I can't do it," you moan, remembering Father Justin's spell. "It's too awful. I won't go!"

Shivering, you slide to the floor in the doorway, staring into the blackness. Maybe the company won't need you after all. Maybe you can just sit here and wait until they come back. Maybe it won't be too long.

Unfortunately for you, the adventure has come to an . . .

END

You find yourself in a large square room. In each of the four walls is a doorway, and above each doorway, a head is painted. Each head has its cheeks puffed out and seems to be blowing.

Suddenly a gust of wind comes through each doorway, extinguishing both torches and plunging you into darkness.

"Drat!" the wizard mutters. He mumbles a few words you don't understand, and the tip of his staff bursts into light, brighter than both torches together.

"Let's hope we don't need to hide from anything," the wizard says sourly, raising his staff high. "This Continual Light Spell I'm using isn't reversible."

As you approach one of the doors, you feel a gust of wind coming from the opening, ruffling your hair.

You continue on to examine each of the doors. As you peer down each passageway, you feel air blowing into the room. One door faces to the north, one faces south, one east, and one west.

"Which way do we go now?" Eric asks, glancing around nervously.

"What do you say, Seventhson?" Lord Bloodstone asks.

"Which way you go is a subject that matters not in the least to me!" the wizard replies with a sneer.

Suddenly you hear the sounds of running feet and clashing metal.

"Wererats!" cries Eric. "We must decide quickly!"

1) The doorway to the north is where you entered. This might be your last chance to turn back! If you choose to go through the north door, turn to page 21.

2) Warm, fragrant air blows from the door to the south. If you want to go that way, turn to page 12.

3) Fresh air comes from the door to the east, but you hear sounds of wererats. If you choose to go that way, turn to page 43.

4) A terrible smell emanates from the door to the west. You hear wererats coming from that direction as well, but if you elect to go that way, turn to page 101.

"We have found two magical objects," Eric cries. "Holy Water and a Sword of Valor. But they were taken away from us."

"Come forward," says the lovely voice.

You approach in awe, feeling peace and goodness surround you. You notice as Eric goes forward that the invisible shield no longer bars his way this time.

You watch as Eric continues to walk up to the tomb. You notice that the lady now holds the cup in one hand and the silver sword in the other. As Eric approaches, her eyes remain closed and she is perfectly motionless.

Eric kneels down beside the tomb reverently. "All my life I have loved you, Blue Lady," he says softly, "even though I knew you only from stories my people told. You, most beautiful, most courageous lady; you who braved the horror so that we might have hope: I honor you and love you with all my heart. Tell me how to break this enchanted sleep."

"You must give me what you value most," the soft voice echoes in the chamber.

"All my wealth and my kingdom are yours," Eric promises fervently. "Everything I have is yours!"

"That is not what you value most," the voice replies coolly. "I must have what you value most."

"What—what do you mean?" Eric asks falteringly.

"Give me your strength and your skill with sword and shield," the lady commands. "Give

these to me freely, and I will be your love until the end of our days on earth."

Eric pales. "I must give up my weapons? My strength?" he protests. "And let you fight my battles?"

"Only then can you be victorious," the Blue Lady murmurs.

"Maybe this is a trap," Eric mutters softly, looking around at you and your companions. "If I give up my weapons, surely we are helpless. What should I do?"

1) "We won't be helpless, Eric," you tell him. "You don't need weapons to be strong." If this is what you truly feel, turn to page 146.

2) "Eric!" you cry. "You're right! We'd be helpless without your strength and skill in battle!" If this is what you believe, then turn to page 54.

"I'm going to open the chest," you decide. "It must have what we need hidden in it. I'll open it carefully, though. Unguarded things are sometimes the most dangerous."

As you study the box, you notice that the decorations are mirror images of each other, divided down the middle by a row of finely carved leaves. You examine the carvings carefully, noting each detail.

"I think I've got it!" you say at last. "See how this flower on the left side has six petals, while the one on the right has seven? And the bird on the left has two eyes. The one on the right has only one. Watch!"

Carefully you touch the seventh petal and the second eye at the same time. Suddenly the lid of the box pops open!

Gingerly you point out the tiny barbs of sharp metal sticking out from the sides of the lid. "If anyone tried to raise the lid without using the secret catch, the barbs would scratch his hands. I'll bet they're poisonous!"

"But what have you found?" Eric asks.

"This!" you breathe and reach for a beautiful velvet cloak. Taking hold of it gently, you remove it from the chest.

"I recognize that!" the Blue Lady cries. "It is Ian Whitestone's Cloak of Invisibility!"

"Is it good or evil?" you ask. But even as you speak the words, you feel warmth and hope beginning to spread through your whole body.

"It is good," the Blue Lady says, smiling. "Put it on, Gregor."

Carefully you drape the cloak around your shoulders, then look up with delight at the astonished faces of Eric and your brother.

"He's gone!" Lord Bloodstone reaches out a hand, frantically pawing the air.

"Just the thing to use to creep past that golem!" you shout in elation.

"But how?" Father Justin asks. "We can't all use the cloak."

You remove the cloak and immediately blink back into sight. "Perhaps I could distract the golem while the rest of you fight it."

"Surely where there's one treasure such as this, there must be more nearby," the Blue Lady says, shaking her head from side to side. "We should not fight yet."

1) Do you want to use the cloak to sneak past the golem while the others fight it? If you do, turn to page 67.

2) Or do you think you should search the west room? If so, turn to page 83.

3) If you have been to the west room before, you know how to get past the golem. Turn to page 112.

4) If all of this seems too dangerous, you could always take what you have and leave by the door you came through. If this is your choice, turn to page 140.

Disgusted with what you've seen, you make up your mind. "If he is my brother, I'm ending the relationship right now!" you snap and jerk off the ring.

"Don't you care what becomes of him?" Father Justin asks gently.

"Frankly, no," you reply arrogantly. "He's a coward who let my mother die alone. And now he's hiding in a wine bottle. I don't care about him, and I don't care about any of you. Why should I? Nobody's ever cared about me," you continue, unable to face the disappointment in Eric's eyes.

"I care, Gregor," Father Justin says with a soft smile.

You look at him and swallow, your eyes clouding.

"I wish you would reconsider, Gregor." The cleric touches your hand gently.

1) If you want to reconsider your decision and accompany your friends on their quest, turn to page 139.

2) But if you truly do not care what becomes of your brother or your new-found friends, then bring your adventure to an end right here, because from now on, you will lead a cold and lonely existence.

THE END

"If we go east, they're sure to follow us," you cry desperately. "Maybe we could hide in that corridor to the south."

"It's worth a try," says Eric.

You hurry over to help your injured brother. Just then, one of the wounded wererats leaps to its feet. Before you can react, the wererat brings its mace down on Lord Bloodstone's head. Screaming in fury, you drive your dagger into the wererat's chest.

You shudder, then turn to your brother. He looks deathly pale, and his face is covered with blood. You kneel beside him, your heart aching. "Can't we do something?" you plead.

"Not here!" Eric kneels beside you, grabs your unconscious brother, and lifts him up. You stand and put one of your brother's arms around your shoulders. Together you carry him into the south corridor. Father Justin limps along behind you, his hand clutching the amulet as he murmurs softly. The wizard starts to follow, then pauses at the entrance to the west passageway.

"This should confuse them for a while," he chuckles. Fumbling in his pouch, he produces a small piece of black fur and a lump of coal. Holding them in his hands, he mutters a few words. The corridor to the west is suddenly plunged into darkness.

"Keep going," Grimpen shouts.

You and Eric drag your unconscious brother down the corridor. Behind you, shouts of astonishment offer proof that Grimpen's

Darkness Spell is having its desired effect.

With the wizard's staff lighting the way, you follow the musty-smelling corridor downhill. Before long, your brother's weight seems to be pulling your arms out of their sockets. Just when you think you can go no farther, the corridor widens into a large, round room.

Immediately you feel peace settle over you. The room is blessedly quiet, except for the soothing, tinkling sound of dripping water. You see a small fountain in the center of the room. A slender stream of water shoots up from the fountain, then cascades down into a circular pool.

On the far wall, what looks like an altar has been carved from solid rock. You see something gleam in the light of the wizard's staff. Gently you and Eric lower Lord Bloodstone down beside the pool as Father Justin investigates the object on the altar.

"Is my brother all right?" you ask Eric.

He leans over Lord Bloodstone. "I'm afraid not, Gregor," Eric answers softly. "One of them must have hit him with a mace. His skull is crushed. I've seen wounds like this before on the field of battle. Blood seeps into the brain. It's a serious wound. I'm afraid there's nothing we can do."

"No!" you cry.

"The Holy Chalice!" Father Justin gasps suddenly. He reaches out and picks up a large, gleaming object from the altar. It's made of gold, encrusted with jewels. He holds it up in the light of the wizard's staff to examine it. "This has long been thought lost!"

"My brother's dying, and all you can think about is that cup!" you shout angrily.

Father Justin looks around. Eric nods briefly, and the cleric's face darkens. He limps to your side, still holding the chalice.

"Can you heal him?" Eric asks.

Father Justin examines Lord Bloodstone carefully before answering. "No. It's a mortal wound. I can cure only light wounds."

You wipe away your tears and kneel down beside your brother. He cries out in pain as his body jerks. Thrashing out, his arm splashes into the pool. Quickly you reach to get it out of the water, when—to your amazement—your brother suddenly sits up!

"What—what happened?" he asks, blinking. "Where are the wererats?"

"He's healed!" you cry.

"It's Holy Water!" gasps Father Justin.

"The wound is gone!" Eric says, pointing.

"Unfortunately we're about to have visitors," Grimpen interjects, totally unimpressed by the miracle. "I hear sounds from the north. The wererats must have found their way through the darkness."

Eric stands and draws his sword. "We must continue heading south."

"Let's take some of this water with us," you suggest, dragging out your water bag. Leaning over to fill it from the pool, however, you are shocked to find that the water runs away from you! No matter how hard you try, you cannot get it into the bag.

"Only a cleric may carry Holy Water," Father Justin explains. He puts his hand down. The water leaps over to him reverently.

"Well, hurry and take some, Father," Eric says as the approaching sounds grow louder.

"But I can't carry both the water and this heavy chalice," Father Justin protests. "And the Holy Chalice must be returned to its place in the chambers of the White Council."

"What purpose does it serve?" you ask.

"It is a symbol," Father Justin replies proudly. "A symbol of holiness."

"The water would be more practical," you mutter. "But I'll carry the chalice." Your fingers touch the gold. With a cry, you draw them back. "It burned me!" you gasp.

"I alone can carry it," Father Justin says, shaking his head. He strokes the chalice lovingly, his eyes aglow with reverence.

"Hurry!" Eric urges.

Father Justin sighs, then looks around as though seeking help.

1) Should you urge Father Justin to take the chalice and leave the Holy Water behind? If this is what you decide, turn to page 90.

2) Or should you try to convince Father Justin to take only the Holy Water? If this is your choice, turn to page 107.

"Father!" you cry, grabbing the cleric's robe. "Help me, please!"

"Rest easy, my son. You are safe." You feel a sense of deep peace and calm flooding through you. The cleric's gentle hand takes your arm, his gentle voice erases the noise and clamor of the crowd. Then the cleric bends down and picks up a stick.

Hugo hoots with laughter. "A crippled cleric can't help you, Gregor. Stand aside, Father, before you get hurt!"

"Thanks anyway, Father," you say slowly. "But this is my fight."

The cleric stands his ground. "Go back to your camp," he says mildly to Hugo. "You cannot harm the boy."

"I warned you!" Hugo lunges forward, his knife flashing.

The cleric makes a quick movement with his hand. "Stick to Snake!" he commands.

Hugo gasps and stares, openmouthed. The stick in the cleric's hand has turned into a slithering snake! Quickly the cleric reaches out and drops it at Hugo's feet.

Hugo's eyes grow large as the snake slithers toward him. The crowd scatters in panic. Repeating all the magic charms he knows, Hugo turns on his heels and runs off down the street.

"Snake to Stick," the cleric says calmly. The snake immediately disappears, to be replaced by the stick you saw earlier. You can only stare in wonder.

"I believe that is your knife, my son," the cleric says, pointing at the knife you saw lying at his feet.

"N-No," you say, swallowing.

"Pick it up," the cleric orders gently.

Confused, you reach down to pick up the knife. You run your hand over the handle gently, admiring the finely carved snake's head and elaborate runes traced on the blade.

"It was a lucky chance that brought you to my aid, Father," you say. "Thank you."

"Luck? I do not believe in luck. No, my son, I was brought here to meet you."

"Brought here!" you exclaim in astonishment. "Who brought you here?"

Please turn to page 55.

"So you have passed all the tests, and now you reach your goal at last," Luben Warlock says. Surprisingly, his voice sounds pleasant and soothing.

He is seated on a throne in the center of a small, round room. Above the throne, a silver moon-shaped opening in the ceiling shines brightly. It is surrounded by seven glowing silver stars. For a few moments all you can do is stare around you in awe.

You return your attention to the figure of the evil sorcerer before you. He smiles at you, and his smile seems more understanding than any you have ever seen before, even Father Justin's. His eyes are brighter than those of the Blue Lady, and he seems stronger and braver than Eric. As he seems to look into your very soul, you want to rush over to absorb his wisdom and knowledge.

Father Justin steps forward resolutely to speak. As you listen, you tell yourself that Luben Warlock is evil, but it's a struggle to believe ill of this handsome man.

"Your charms do not work on me, Luben Warlock," Father Justin says calmly. "I have been sent by the White Council to rid this land of your evil curse, and I will do so, even if it means my death."

"How you misunderstand me, Father!" Luben says sorrowfully, and you feel a flash of pity for him. "I do not want to kill you—or any of these bold adventurers. I desire only your happiness. Take the magical objects you have discovered and leave in safety. Take the Cloak of Invisibility, the Sword of Valor, the Holy Water, and poor Ian's spellbook." He leans forward, spreading out his hands. "I can give you a truly happy ending. You deserve it! Anything you want—just ask me for it!"

"Anything?" you repeat. "Even removing the curse?"

"If that is your idea of a happy ending, that is what I will grant," Luben Warlock says with a shrug.

"What if we don't believe this story?" Eric growls. "What then?"

"Then you will find me a formidable opponent, and you will fight a battle you most certainly won't survive."

Luben Warlock looks at you, his eyes gleaming. "What about it, Gregor?" he asks softly. "Which do you choose? The happy ending—or its unthinkable alternative?"

"Remember, Gregor," whispers the voice of the Blue Lady in your mind. "His words are twisted. Consider his real meaning well!"

1) Do you choose the happy ending? After all, Luben Warlock has promised to lift the curse from the land. If so, turn to page 144.

2) Or do you choose to fight Luben Warlock, even though defeat seems almost certain? If you choose to fight, turn to page 153.

Feeling the comforting pressure of your knife tucked safely inside your sash, you take a deep breath and lunge backward suddenly, knocking the man holding you to the floor. Then you jam your elbow into his stomach, leaving him gasping for breath.

Quickly you regain your feet and lash out with one leg just as another man leaps for you. Your foot catches him in the kneecap. Roaring in pain, he staggers across the room.

You pull your knife and face the third man. He glances nervously at his two friends, one rolling in pain on the floor and the other clutching his injured knee. Drunkenly he returns his gaze to the gleaming knife blade. Then he backs away, his hands in the air.

"You and your friends clear out!" growls the innkeeper as he comes up from the cellar, a dusty bottle in his hand. "Important guests are coming. I don't want any trouble."

One by one, the men limp out, muttering and groaning.

Breathing hard, you return to the table.

"Well done, Gregor!" Eric exclaims. "I'm beginning to think Father Justin has chosen another companion for our quest wisely. Will you join us, Gregor?"

"I—I don't know anything about you or your quest," you reply with gypsy caution. "What is it that you seek?"

"You, Gregor, will seek something you have sought all your life. You will seek yourself," Father Justin answers softly.

"Clerics!" you think in disgust. "They never give you a straight answer when a riddle will do." The practical side of you says to leave now, before you get into any more trouble. But the adventurer in you whispers to stay just a little longer to find out more about this mysterious quest! Which side do you listen to?

1) If you decide to stay, turn to page 120.

2) If you decide to leave, turn to page 135.

"I think we should let the wizard try his trick on the wererats and go back to the Room of the Four Winds," you say.

"Go ahead, wizard," Eric says grimly.

The wizard leans forward, searching the floor, as the wererat voices grow closer.

"This is no time to look for dust!" Eric shouts. "Let's get out of here!"

"Ah-ha!" the wizard cries and comes up holding a live cricket in one hand.

Before your stunned gaze, Grimpen pops the cricket into his mouth, makes a curious hand motion, swallows, then chants a few words. You gag and look away.

Suddenly you no longer hear the wererat voices. In their place, you hear snoring!

"I've put them to sleep," the wizard explains. "But they won't stay that way for long. We've got to get past them in a hurry!"

"What about my brother?" you ask.

"I can help him." Father Justin lays a hand on your brother's head and murmurs the words of the Cure Light Wounds Spell.

Immediately your brother's eyes open. The wound on his head is gone!

"Come on," Eric urges. "We don't have any time to waste!"

You help your brother back down the corridor to the west. Soon you find yourselves back in the Room of the Four Winds.

Please turn to page 23 and choose a different direction.

"I think we should try the west door," you say. "We should look for something to help us face whatever's behind the north door. If the symbols do mean that good can eclipse evil, perhaps we'll find something there."

You walk resolutely to the west door and reach for the handle. "Ouch!" you cry out as your hand meets something hard and invisible. You wring your hand in pain, shaking your head. "We can't go that way," you say.

"It's a force field," Grimpen Seventhson says, tapping it with his staff. "Try the east door."

"YOU try it," you say.

The wizard walks over and touches the handle of the east door with his staff. Suddenly there's a flash of light, and the staff is knocked out of the wizard's hand!

"I guess we won't be going that way either," Eric says grimly. "We're being forced to go north."

"Not me! I'm getting out of here!" shouts your brother. He walks over to the south door, but as he approaches, it slams shut in his face.

"Well, north it is," you mutter.

Please turn to page 60.

"There's fresh air coming from this direction!" you cry, pointing to the east door. "There must be an opening to the outside."

"Yes, but I hear wererats, too," Father Justin says.

"If so, I'd rather face them in the open," Eric replies grimly, his sword in his hand. "Come on, Lord Bloodstone. Now's your chance to prove your courage!"

"It is a chance to prove my stupidity," Lord Bloodstone says with a shrug. "But why not?"

The two of them move cautiously through the east entrance. You follow, your golden knife warm in your hand. Father Justin limps after you, chanting softly. Last comes the wizard, holding his staff high to light the way.

The corridor curves slightly, bending to the right for a long distance. Noises from the approaching wererats become louder and louder. Suddenly bright light appears at the end of the corridor, nearly blinding you.

"It leads outdoors!" you cry. "Only a few more yards and we'll be out of here!" Then you see two large, towering boulders. Their shapes seem horribly familiar, like something out of a long-forgotten nightmare.

"The Fanged Rocks," gasps Bloodstone.

"Wererats!" yells Eric. A troop of wererats appears in the corridor.

"Well, lookee here," snarls the leader. "Here we was, searching for dinner. And here it comes—on the hoof, so to speak. Have at 'em, lads!"

Before you can think, the wererats charge into your party's midst. You see the flash of Eric's sword, then hear a scream as a wererat falls to the ground. You glance toward your brother. Lord Bloodstone draws his foil—a slender, fencing weapon. He stands staring at the wererats, breathing hard. Sweat makes his black curls shine.

"Fight!" Eric yells as more wererats swarm into the room.

You see Lord Bloodstone gulp. He shakes his head, then begins to back up. Two wererats screech in glee and rush toward him as he bumps up against the wall of the cavern.

"Stop!" you yell.

The knife in your hand comes alive as you attack the wererats from behind. As you fight furiously, you notice your brother is bleeding from a cut on the forehead. Finally the wererats fall back in confusion and disappear down a corridor.

But just as you think you've won, Father Justin's voice shatters your hopes. "More wererats, coming from the west!" he shouts.

"We've got to make a break for it!" Eric shouts as he bashes a wererat on the head, then shoves it aside with his foot. "It seems clear to the south, where the first group came from."

"Or we could continue east and get out of these cursed catacombs." Lord Bloodstone leans against the cavern wall, his face covered with blood.

"Or we could surprise the wererats in the corridor," offers the wizard, leaning comfortably on his staff, "then go back west, the way we came. I have a trick up my sleeve for them."

1) Do you want to get out of the catacombs? If so, go east by turning to page 63.

2) Do you think it is safe down the south corridor, since you have apparently routed the wererats? If you think so, turn to page 30.

3) Or would you rather follow the wizard's advice and face the wererats in the corridor, then go west? If so, turn to page 41.

"I'm sure it's a trap," you say. "There's noth ing guarding it, but things left unguarded are frequently the most dangerous. I'm not going to touch it!"

"I agree," seconds Eric. "Let's get out of here. We're just going to have to face the golem on our own."

"I'm not sure you're making the right deci- sion," the Blue Lady says, looking back sadly at the chest as you leave the room. "I had the feeling there was something quite valuable inside. . . ."

"Well, we can always come back later," Eric reasons aloud.

"No, you can't!" you hear an evil voice laugh. Suddenly there is a loud blast, and you are hurled against the west door by the force of the magic spell. Father Justin is knocked flat. Eric skids across the floor and crashes into a wall. Your brother hurtles into you, squashing you against the door.

"Look!" you manage to yell as soon as you can regain your breath.

The Blue Lady and Grimpen, unaffected by the blast, are now beginning to glow with a hideous red light!

"No!" Eric cries, staggering to his feet.

"Stop!" The Blue Lady holds up her hand in warning. "Don't come near. It is Luben War- lock's magic. There is no hope for us. You must try to escape. Farewell!"

Before your eyes, she begins to fade. Grim- pen appears to be struggling mightily. With a loud gasp, he hurls his staff toward you, and it falls at your feet.

"There's . . . one more spell . . . left!" he gasps. "The Teleport Spell. Use it, fools!" With his last word, Grimpen Seventhson disappears into thin air.

Numbly you pick up the still glowing staff and look around you. Eric has collapsed, weeping bitterly. Your brother has his arm around him, trying to comfort him.

"We've got to get out of here!" Father Justin shouts as he crawls toward you. "Use the staff, Gregor!"

"I can't remember the command word!" you cry, staring at the staff wildly.

"Think! Grimpen used it to teleport us from the Tomb of the Blue Lady!"

"I know . . . " you say, closing your eyes and trying to remember. . . .

1) If you remember the word the wizard used, say it and you will be teleported safely out of the catacombs and back to town.

2) Unfortunately, if you can't remember the word, this is . . .

THE END

You help the others wake Lord Bloodstone and drag your brother to the door of the inn. One of the men-at-arms helps the lord stagger back to Bloodstone Manor.

Meanwhile, Eric buys provisions for your quest at the inn, divides them up, and hands you each a pack and a water bag to carry.

"So you think we'll live until dinnertime?" cackles the wizard.

Eric glares at him, then turns and stalks out of the inn. You and Father Justin follow, with Grimpen trailing, still laughing.

As you walk, people stare at you and your companions in the streets. You notice all of them are ragged and gaunt with sickness and poverty. The buildings you pass are falling into ruin. You notice that the marketplace is closed already, though it is not yet midmorning. What little food there was has all been sold. You feel something else is strange, but you can't quite put your finger on it. Suddenly it occurs to you.

"Where are all the children?" you ask Father Justin suddenly.

He sighs deeply. "There are no children anymore, Gregor. That is part of the curse. No children are born here anymore. There is no change. No one in this town can leave. If they try, they suddenly find themselves teleported back. They can do nothing except grow old and die without hope."

"Who started the curse?" you ask, horrified.

"I'll answer that." It is the wizard's voice. He

puts his twisted hand on your arm, and you slow your pace to match his.

"A wizards' conclave was held here years ago. Wizards from all over the world attended—good wizards as well as evil. All sought one goal—to bring this kingdom prosperity. But no one could agree on how to bring this about. Arguments raged, becoming more and more dangerous. Finally the head of one order was found murdered by sorcery. After that, it was a nightmare!"

"How do you know this?" you ask, shivering.

"Because I was there," the wizard hisses.

You stare at the wizard in astonishment.

"Yes," Grimpen says, nodding. "I was only an apprentice then, but my master was destroyed. They were all destroyed. Only I escaped, probably because I was too young to take seriously. I hid, terrified, and watched the final battle between the last survivors— the Blue Lady and the evil Luben Warlock."

"What happened?" you ask with a shiver.

"Luben Warlock put a powerful curse on this town. Instead of prosperity, the town would have nothing but poverty. Since the Blue Lady was unable to undo his curse, she added a condition—that a group of heroes, if they remain true to their quest and to each other, can find a way to remove the curse."

As the wizard talks, you round a corner and realize you have left the squalid town behind and are now walking along what was once a long, tree-lined carriage drive. It, like everything else, has fallen into ruin. Everywhere trees are dead or dying. Most of the cobblestones are missing or broken. You stumble into a hole and Grimpen steadies you. "What did Luben Warlock do then?" you ask.

"The evil wizard was furious. He filled the catacombs with deadly traps," interjects Father Justin. "Then he summoned all manner of evil creatures to live in the catacombs. That was his last act, however. His power drained, he was imprisoned by the Blue Lady."

"Weakened herself, the Blue Lady could do only one more spell," Eric continues. "She sacrificed herself, leaving her spirit behind to aid those who might try to end the curse. My people believe she is there still."

Carefully he brings out a small portrait and shows it to you. The painting shows a woman of rare beauty. You know now why Eric is willing to risk his life to enter the catacombs.

"Here we are," Father Justin announces.

You look up. Like all the other buildings in town, Bloodstone Manor is slowly decaying. It might once have been great, but now it only fills you with dread and foreboding.

Lord Bloodstone waits for you at the entrance with his men-at-arms. "After we are inside," he says to the captain, "lock and bar the doors. No one else is to enter. We are going into the Endless Catacombs. If we do not return, pay off the men and dismiss them."

"Yes, my lord," the captain replies, paling.

"Then farewell!" The lord rings a bellpull, and the doors to Bloodstone Manor swing open. When you are all inside, Bloodstone slams the huge door closed, and you hear the sound of the door being barred shut.

Bloodstone leads the way across a dark hallway to a staircase. Beneath the staircase is a small wooden door. He halts, brings out an ancient key, and fits it into the lock. Slowly the door creaks open. Brushing aside cobwebs, he says with a crooked smile, "The catacombs, gentlemen. Down these stairs we will come to the bricked-up wall."

"The company must be true to each other," Grimpen Seventhson chortles. "I say this quest is doomed before it begins!"

"I fear the same thing," Eric says grimly. "I refuse to go if the wizard goes."

"But we need a magic-user!" Father Justin pleads. "You must have faith, Eric!"

"I say we find another wizard." Eric glowers at Seventhson, who laughs strangely.

"We must go now!" Father Justin repeats desperately. "Don't you see what is happening? The curse is already at work—on us!"

1) If you agree with Eric and want to wait till your party finds another wizard, turn to page 87.

2) If you agree with Father Justin and want to let Grimpen Seventhson come with your party, turn to page 14.

"I can't give up my weapons and my strength!" Eric declares. "I believe this is a trap. You are merely an illusion!"

"Is that your decision?" the voice asks.

"It is," Eric states firmly.

"Then I am sorry, for you have failed in your quest. Since you faced such great peril, I will return all of you to your former place and time. But you will have no memory of me or of your quest. Farewell."

Before you can even cry out, you find yourself standing in a filthy street, staring up at a sign that has ten swords on it. Blinking, you try to remember how you got here.

As you stare at the tavern, two figures emerge. One is a cleric, the other a handsome fighter. They seem vaguely familiar somehow. . . . You listen to their conversation.

"It's driving me crazy, Father Justin," the fighter is saying. "I know I've lost something important, but I can't remember what!"

"I know, Eric," the cleric replies, shaking his head. "I have the same feeling."

The two continue on down the street. You shrug and enter the tavern. Here a nobleman lies snoring on a table, an empty flagon near his hand. A cunning-looking wizard stares at you with gleaming eyes.

Deciding you don't like the look of this place, you back out of the tavern and head down the street. For you, the adventure . . .

NEVER BEGAN!

The cleric smiles mysteriously, removes the amulet from around his neck, and raises it toward the sky. "This brought me to help you," he replies.

You frown, then back away nervously. The cleric takes a step toward you. You see now that he has a twisted foot, which drags along the ground when he walks, forcing him to walk with a limp. As you examine the cleric, he in turn is examining you, taking in every part of your gaily colored gypsy clothing from your stout leather boots to the pouch that holds your tarot cards and the thieving tools Hugo forces you to carry.

"My name is Father Justin," the cleric says finally. "And you?"

"They call me Gregor," you say.

"WHO calls you Gregor?" the cleric asks, smiling. "Isn't that your name?"

"It's not my real name," you say, flushing. "It's a name the gypsies gave me. I don't even know my real name. I've lived with the gypsies since I was small."

"Well, Gregor, may peace go with you from now on." Father Justin nods and seems about to turn away when he stiffens suddenly and grabs your left hand. "Where did you get this?" he demands, his voice no longer gentle.

Startled, you look down at the ring on your finger. "It's mine!" you cry. "I didn't steal it! The gypsies found it hanging on a golden chain around my neck when they rescued me from the wererats."

"Indeed?" the cleric says with great interest. "You were attacked by wererats?"

"It happened when I was only three," you say, swallowing. The memories are vague but frightening. "The wererats killed my mother before the gypsies came and fought them off."

"And that was near here, was it not?" the cleric pursues eagerly.

"Yes . . . near the Fanged Rocks" you reply, eyeing the cleric suspiciously. "How did you know that?"

"I'm surprised the gypsies let you keep the ring," the cleric murmurs, ignoring your question.

"The old woman told them it would bring a curse on whoever touched it. She said it was a lucky charm, meant for me alone." You shrug. "It's not very pretty or even very valuable. Hugo calls it a bloodstone."

"Yes . . . a bloodstone." The cleric nods, staring intently at the green gem. Red lines run through it like blood veins, giving the jewel its name. "And its value depends on many things."

"What things?" you ask eagerly. If you had money, you could run away from the gypsies and start life all over.

"Come with me," the cleric offers suddenly. "I know some people who will be interested in your ring."

"Where?" you ask, suspicious once more.

"Not far. Look, you can see it from here."

Your eyes follow in the direction he is point-

ing, down a dark, dingy street. There, at the
far end, above the road, swings a half-broken
sign. You've never been taught to read, but
you recognize the picture: ten swords. The Inn
of the Ten Swords! You shudder. It's an evil
omen. In the tarot cards, ten swords stand for
death and destruction.

You turn back to the cleric. He seems gentle
enough, but not all clerics are good. Some follow the ways of Chaos. You know he is powerful, too, remembering the Snake Spell. Yet
this cleric obviously knows something about
your ring. There might be someone at the inn
who is interested in buying it.

1) If you decide to follow the cleric to the
   Inn of Ten Swords, turn to page 75.

2) If you decide not to trust the cleric, turn
   to page 103.

"See that place up ahead where the corridor widens?" Eric asks, pointing. "When we get there, fall back into the shadows. We'll ambush them from there."

As you creep forward, you see what the fighter's sharp eyes had noticed in the darkness ahead. The corridor widens into a small room. There is an opening at the far end that leads west. You move into the shadows and crouch, waiting. Grimpen Seventhson enters the room, his staff glowing in the darkness.

"Douse that light!" Eric hisses.

"I can't!" the wizard snaps. "The Continual Light Spell can't be reversed!"

"Oh, wonderful!" you groan.

Suddenly your brother rushes forward. Snatching the plumed hat from his head, he pulls it down over the staff. The light is extinguished.

"Keep it that way until the wererats get here!" Eric orders as the wizard, grumbling, moves hurriedly into a corner.

You hear the sound of wererat voices right outside the opening.

"Don't shove!" one shouts.

"Well, quit trying to crowd ahead of me! Why're you in such a hurry to eat, anyway?"

"I still don't believe you rodents heard anything down here."

They enter the chamber and begin to cross it. They're nearly halfway across when Eric leaps out from the shadows and brings his sword crashing down on the head of one.

You run forward, your knife glowing brightly. Quickly you dispose of a wererat who is about to swing its battleax at Eric's head. The wizard has removed Lord Bloodstone's hat from his staff, and its glow fills the chamber with light. You hear Father Justin begin to chant, and you feel your spirits lift as his words fill you with hope.

You glance at your brother. Lord Bloodstone stands against the far wall, his face ashen. His sword—a slender fencing foil—hangs useless at his side.

You have no time to worry about him, though. Another wererat swings its mace in a long arc straight at your head. You duck and hurl yourself into its thick body, knocking the wind out of it. You tumble to the floor and roll around, struggling, the wererat trying to bash you with its mace while you search for an opening in its armor to drive home your knife.

Suddenly you feel a hand dragging you up and back. Eric coolly shoves you aside and finishes off the wererat. The room becomes silent, littered with wererat bodies. Eric glances at your brother in disgust but says nothing. You feel yourself blush and avoid looking at your brother.

Without a word, Eric leads the way out of the room and through the door leading west. Everyone follows, with Lord Bloodstone trailing along miserably at the rear.

Please turn to page 141.

You all crowd around the north door. Hesitantly you reach toward it. It feels cool to the touch. You listen carefully. "I hear something," you whisper. "It sounds like some sort of a heavy weight being moved around."

Warily you press on the door. To your surprise, it opens easily. Eric steps through, his sword drawn. The wizard shines his staff in the darkness beyond.

"I am the Guardian!" booms a powerful voice. "Who goes there?"

"An iron golem!" Eric gasps in horror.

Now you see the fearsome creature, standing at attention at the far end of the corridor. Magic light gleams from its armor and its huge sword. It's almost twelve feet tall, and its helm brushes the high ceiling. You have never seen anything so terrifying!

"We come in peace!" Eric shouts.

"I guard the door. No one may pass!" the golem intones in a deep voice. "Death to anyone who attempts to pass!"

"I'd say that's pretty clear." Lord Bloodstone licks his dry lips.

"The golem was placed there by the evil wizards," explains the Blue Lady. "The good wizards must have left some means to defeat it, in order to maintain the balance of good and evil. I think we should explore the other rooms."

"But we don't know what we're looking for!" Eric argues. "And there isn't much time. The wererats are bound to be back sooner or later. I say we fight the golem."

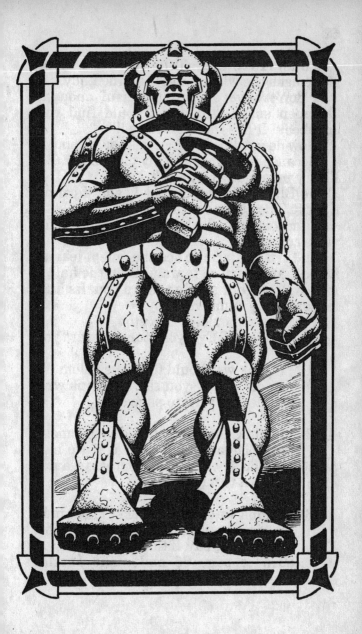

"Can you cast a spell on it?" Lord Blood-stone asks the wizard and the Blue Lady.

"I don't have a spell powerful enough," Grimpen snaps. "If only I could find that spellbook! It has the spell I need!"

"How do you know?" Eric asks suspiciously.

"Because it belonged to my old master. But I'll try magic, if you insist."

The Blue Lady shakes her head. "I cannot fight it. I possess no attack spells."

"I am coming to deal with you!" the golem's voice rumbles.

You turn in alarm to see the golem leaving its post and starting to walk down the hall. It moves slowly but surely toward you, its huge feet shuffling cumbersomely.

"I think we should—" You stop.

"Should what?" Everyone turns toward you.

1) "I think we should fight the golem. We can defeat it!" you say. If this is what you decide, turn to page 96.

2) "I think Grimpen should use a magic spell. Then we can fight it if we need to," you say. If this is what you want to do, turn to page 136.

3) "I think we should go back. There must be some way to get into those other rooms!" you say. If this is your decision, turn to page 65 and make another choice.

"My brother's hurt! We've got to get him out of here!" you cry. Even as you speak, Lord Bloodstone collapses. Eric catches him as he falls. The sound of the approaching wererats grows louder.

"This way!" Eric shouts. He runs east, out through the cave opening, toward the Fanged Rocks.

You hesitate. You fear the Fanged Rocks almost as much as you fear staying in the catacombs. Then you hear the wererats screeching from very near and you decide.

You put your arm around Father Justin and help him limp out through the opening. The wizard stays behind, leaning on his staff.

"Hurry, Seventhson!" Father Justin twists around to yell.

"What's to prevent the wererats from coming after us?" the wizard snaps. He raises his staff and begins to speak.

"No!" Father Justin screams, but it's already too late.

A huge ball of fire explodes from the wizard's staff and barrels down the corridor. You hear sounds of panic from the terror-stricken wererats.

"Run!" the wizard yells, diving out of the cave entrance.

You fling yourself forward just as there is another deafening explosion. Then you hear nothing but the sound of crashing rock. For a moment, all you see is a huge cloud of dust. When it clears, you see that the cave entrance is completely blocked by huge boulders. Then all is quiet.

"Well," Eric says, staring back at the cave, "you've done it now, wizard. We'll never be able to get back in!"

"My, my." Grimpen strokes his beard sadly. "I did misjudge that spell a bit, didn't I?"

"We shouldn't have run," Father Justin sighs. "We should have stayed and fought."

You go to your brother, who lies with his head resting on a clump of soft grass. You brush back your brother's dark hair to examine his wound. It doesn't look too serious. The old woman has a potion that will cure him.

"I'm sorry, Gregor," he groans. "It's my fault. I'll never be anything but a coward!"

"No," you say, shaking your head firmly. "You didn't want to come. We made you."

As you sit there, the ground is rocked by yet another explosion, and a cloud of debris rises into the air.

"It'll be a long, long time before anyone can get into the catacombs now," Eric says grimly. "Bloodstone Manor just blew up."

"I'm—I'm glad it's gone," Lord Bloodstone sighs. You know he's sad, but he seems calm. "But what will we live on, Gregor?"

"There's always the tarot cards," you say with a grin, wondering how your brother will like life as a gypsy.

THE END

"We've got to go back to those other rooms!" you say. "There's no way we can defeat that monster without help!"

"You may be sure of it," the Blue Lady says.

"I suppose you're right, Gregor," Eric admits, then turns to face the golem. "Return to your watch, golem!" he shouts. "We will trouble you no further for now!"

You all crowd back out the door and Eric slams it shut. You put your ear to the door and hear the sound of heavy footsteps moving away from you. The golem has returned to its post.

"Now what?" Father Justin asks.

"We must choose another door," you reply, studying the strange symbols.

1) Do you choose the door to the east, which shows the moon obscured by clouds? It might mean something is hidden there. If you do, turn to page 93.

2) Do you choose the door to the west, showing the moon in eclipse? It could stand for good eclipsing evil. If so, turn to page 83.

3) Or do you choose the south door and try to escape? If this is your choice, turn to page 140.

"I was going to steal a purse from a fat nobleman," you explain quickly, "when a black cat jumped out right in front of me!"

Quickly you embroider your lie, watching in relief as Hugo slowly lowers his fist. "The cat crossed my path, spitting and yowling and staring straight up at me. What could I do? I wasn't going to try for the man's money after such an evil omen! I guess my luck is ruined for the day."

You step backward, slip on a rotten cabbage leaf, and fall flat in a pile of refuse. "See?" You raise your hands helplessly.

"You're right," Hugo agrees, then mutters a magic charm to ward off evil. "Stay away from me, boy! Go back to the camp. Read fortunes with the women!"

Making a wide, careful circle around you, Hugo heads down the alley for the marketplace. You've escaped a beating for today—but what about tomorrow?

"I could run away," you think, "and live in some other city." You glance around the smelly, dingy alley. "No," you think with a shudder. "Better a gypsy's life in the open air than trapped in some accursed town. Maybe the old woman can think of some way to save me from becoming a thief."

You make your way out of the city to the gypsy camp. Without your even knowing it, your adventure has come to an . . .

END

"I'll distract the golem," you say eagerly. "Then you attack it when it isn't looking."

"All right," Eric agrees. "I'll call to it from the end of the hall. When it comes after me, you sneak past, then taunt it from behind. When it turns, we'll attack."

"Right!" Once more you don the Cloak of Invisibility, then hurry back to the north door.

Taking a deep breath, Eric opens the door and enters the hallway. "Golem, let us pass!" he shouts. "We come in peace!"

"I am the Guardian!" the iron golem thunders, rising to its feet and beginning to move down the hall. "Who goes there?"

"It is I, Eric, Prince of the Windswept Dunes! Let us pass, or you will have to fight us!" Eric announces, drawing his sword.

"I look forward to the fight," the golem rumbles, raising its weapon. You gulp.

"Go, Gregor!" Eric whispers.

Gathering your courage, you start down the corridor, hoping the cloak is working. The eyes of the golem seem to be staring right at you as it thunders down the hallway, but it clomps right past you, unseeing.

"Whew!" you gasp. Then you begin to shout the first thing that pops into your head: "Hey, Rusty! Over here!"

"RUSTY!" The golem stops and turns its head, its eyes glaring like burning coals.

"Hey, you big hitching post!" you scream. "You should be out front. There's no place to park the horses!"

"I cannot see you, but I will crush you like a bug!" The iron golem begins to turn around in the narrow corridor.

As it does so, you see Eric and Lord Bloodstone race from the end of the hallway, their weapons drawn. The Sword of Valor bites deeply into the golem's leg, but Eric's sword merely glances off with a loud clang.

The golem pays no attention to his attackers and continues to search for you, muttering angrily under its breath.

"We can't fight this thing, Gregor!" Eric shouts, wringing his hands. You know they sting from the blow against the iron creature.

"This is one heck of a time to decide that!" you shout.

"Get out, Gregor!" Eric calls. He and your brother begin to back toward the door.

"All right," you shout back, gritting your teeth. "I'll try."

The golem is almost upon you now, though it obviously still can't see you. It stamps its feet in frustration as it searches for you. Just as one huge foot raises right over you, you scamper between its legs and bump into Eric at the door.

"Let's try the west room," you gasp, breathing heavily.

"Good idea," Eric states, slamming the door shut.

Please turn to page 83.

"This is crazy!" you think. "I'm not going to stay here and get pounded into pulp by these bullies!"

Wriggling free of the man's grasp, you drop to the floor and scoot between the legs of the drunken ruffians. Before their befuddled brains can figure out what has happened, you regain your feet and dash out the tavern door.

You are thankful to have escaped not only from the drunks but also from the cleric and his mysterious friend. Hearing footsteps, you begin to run once more. You still have the knife and your ring. Surely both of them together will buy you enough to live on.

Pausing a moment, you look back at the Inn of the Ten Swords. Truly it is an ill-omened place! And leaving it has brought your adventure to an . . .

END

You know that Father Justin seems to think there's something evil in that room. Maybe you should let Eric try for the sword, you decide. You stand back as Eric strides forward into the room.

"No!" Father Justin shouts, shaking his head and clutching his amulet. "Don't enter that room!"

Suddenly you know why. A terrifying figure rises up behind Eric.

"A wraith!" shouts Father Justin. You stare in horror. The wraith is blacker than darkness, yet it glows with a chilling, unearthly light. It floats slowly toward Eric, its hand outstretched.

"Eric!" you scream. The warrior turns and falls backward at the sight of the wraith, fumbling for his sword.

"Ordinary weapons won't work against the undead!" Father Justin gasps. "Use your magic knife, Gregor!"

"Turn it, cleric!" the wizard snaps.

"I can't! There's some sort of evil power preventing me," Father Justin says, trembling. "I can't enter that room!"

You take a deep breath and draw your knife. Just as you run forward, the wraith lays its chilling hand on Eric's shoulder! "Living man," it whispers in a foul voice, "I hate your warm blood. Now you will join me in the world of the undead!"

Eric cries out in pain and falls to the floor. You leap forward, your magic knife in your

hand, but before you can strike, the wraith turns to face you.

"Another warm, living body!" it screeches gleefully. It floats toward you. You stand paralyzed with fear.

"Get the sword, Gregor!" Father Justin shouts. "It's made of silver. It can kill the wraith!"

But you can't move. Frantically you look around and see your brother in the doorway.

"Lord Bloodstone!" you plead. "Help me!"

You can tell from your brother's pale face and trembling body that he is desperately frightened. Can he muster the courage to come to your aid?

1) If you have faith in your brother, then call him once more to come and help. Turn to page 128.

2) If you feel you should have known better than to ask for help from your cowardly brother, turn to page 84.

"I don't think we should drink the wine," you caution.

"Why not, Gregor?" Father Justin asks as he dusts off a bottle. "It is plainly elvish wine—look at these runes."

"I know, but—" You hesitate, afraid that they will laugh at you. "Hugo used to say that I shouldn't eat or drink anything unless I knew exactly where it came from." You blush. "It was part of my training to be a thief."

"Sound advice nonetheless," says Eric. "You should know that, Father, after all our adventures together."

"Yes, I suppose so. . . ." Father Justin sighs and places the bottle back in the wine rack. "But elvish wine could have been such a help to us!"

Your brother reaches out for the bottle, but you grab his hand. "You have me now, my lord," you say softly. "You don't need that. I have some sweet water in my pack."

You feel his hand shake, then he draws it back. "Very well," he says, smiling crookedly. "Let us try your 'sweet water.'"

"We know where the wine is," Grimpen says. "We can always return if necessary."

Eric glowers at the wizard, then changes the subject. "And now we had best go back the way we came, since there seems to be no other way out of this room."

Please return to page 23 and choose another direction.

"The Room of the Four Winds!" you cry. "How will we ever get back there?"

"Maybe the kobolds will open the doors for us," Eric says grimly.

"Stand alongside me and keep your hands on my robes," Grimpen Seventhson orders suddenly. All of you look at him, unmoving. "I can teleport us to the Room of the Four Winds," the wizard continues, "the room we started from. Then we simply need to choose a different direction. One is bound to lead us to the other object."

"Very well," Eric agrees reluctantly. "I suppose we have no choice."

You move near the wizard and grasp his robe. The wizard raises his staff and speaks a single, harsh word: "XIT!" There is a bright flash, and . . .

Please turn to page 23 and choose a direction different from the one you chose to get here.

"All right. I'll come with you," you say, shrugging. "I can sell my ring, if you think they'd be interested in buying it."

"Perhaps . . ." the cleric says, limping off down the street.

You follow slowly behind him, and before long you stand beneath the creaking sign. The cleric enters the inn without pausing. The place smells of burned food and stale wine. You hesitate. He looks back and beckons.

Shivering, you enter the Inn of the Ten Swords, giving your ring a quick rub to protect you against evil. Your misgivings increase as you step into the smothering dimness. A fire sputters in the grate but gives off little warmth. The fading sunlight turns to gray as it filters through the dirty windows.

Three drunken men sit hunched over heavy mugs. "Gypsy trash," one belches as you walk by.

The cleric takes no notice of any of this, however. Dragging his crippled foot, he limps through the smoky room toward a high-backed wooden booth, where a figure waits, shrouded in shadow. You follow close behind the cleric, your hand on the hilt of your knife.

"Greetings, Eric," the cleric says softly as you near the booth. "It's been many years, my friend."

"Greetings, Father Justin," the shadowy figure replies. His voice is deep and strong. "The years have been many, and they have been hard. Still, now I have hope."

"There is hope indeed." Father Justin seats himself in the booth, then grasps his friend by the hand. He motions for you to join them. You draw up a chair and perch on its edge, nervous and afraid.

"Why have you brought this gypsy?" Eric stares at you from beneath the hood of his cape. You see two amazingly clear blue eyes beneath fair blond hair. His face is stern and weathered, as if from many journeys. He looks at you keenly but does not seem favorably impressed.

"I have my reasons for bringing him," Father Justin replies mildly. "Introduce yourself to Eric, my son."

"I am called Gregor," you answer.

"Just another gypsy thief," Eric says with a shrug.

You flush angrily.

"Easy, Gregor," Father Justin admonishes. He rests his hand on your arm, and you notice that his touch has a calming influence on you.

Eric laughs scornfully. "You always were softhearted, Father. A clever thief might be of some use to us, but not a gypsy. They're noted for their loyalty to the side of Chaos."

"Our loyalty is to ourselves!" you answer hotly. Before you can continue, however, a huge hand grabs you from behind and drags you from your chair.

"Get out of this tavern, gypsy trash!" Beery breath gags you as a huge man holds you squirming in his grasp. Two friends, equally

as drunk and as large, loom behind him. Eric
does not seem inclined to help you, and Father
Justin merely watches in silence. You realize
they are waiting to see how you handle the situation.

How WILL you handle this situation? You
think you might be able to take on these three
bullies in a fight, especially since they are
drunk. But then again, they're awfully big!
You might try talking your way out of this, or
you could simply run away—though that
would mean you'd never see Father Justin or
Eric again.

1) If you want to try to talk your way out
   of this predicament, turn to page 130.

2) If you prefer to fight the three men,
   turn to page 39.

3) Or if you decide to try to escape, turn to
   page 69.

"Elvish wine!" you think. Though elves have disappeared from your country, you've heard stories of the magical powers of elvish wine. It is said to increase strength and stamina, even help overcome fear. Furthermore, it isn't supposed to be intoxicating.

"Do you think it's real, Father?" you ask.

"I believe it is," the cleric replies, dusting off the bottle. "Look at these runes. They're certainly elvish in design."

"They are indeed," Eric admits, examining them closely. "But we should hurry. Those wererats may decide to come this way."

Your brother already has the bottle uncorked. Eagerly you cup your hands. The wine flows into them, pale and fragrant.

Slowly you sip the delicious liquid. It fills you with sweet warmth. Thirstily you gulp down the rest from your hands.

"It must be elvish wine, Father!" you cry. "I'm not afraid anymore!" Your brother drinks, then passes the bottle to Eric. Soon all of you are sitting on the floor, listening to Eric tell stories of his adventures.

When the wererats come in, you roar with laughter. Eric gets up to do his impression of two wererats fighting over a dead dog.

"Hey!" you giggle as one of the wererats pokes you with its sword. "That tickles!"

Until the effects of the wine wear off, it looks as if your adventure has come to an . . .

END

"I'm staying!" you announce firmly. "If the rest of you have enough courage and faith, then so do I. Besides, the Blue Lady needs us!"

"I'll stay with you, brother," Lord Bloodstone says with a thin smile.

"Oh, very well," the wizard says sourly. "We'll all die a horrible death. I suppose you know that."

"You don't have to stay," you tell him.

"I'm not stupid enough to go out there alone," Grimpen replies, glaring at you. "If Luben Warlock killed all of you, he'd only come after me next. Better to die quickly."

"Are you staying?" the Blue Lady calls.

"Yes!" you answer loudly.

"Then come and stand near me—quickly!" she orders.

You run forward and stand near her, facing the evil Warlock, who has his eyes closed now, putting the finishing touches on his spell.

"Don't be frightened." She places one hand on your shoulder, and it feels cool and comforting. "He will raise his hand in a moment, and four fireballs will shoot out from his fingertips. The air will be filled with flame and smoke, but it will not harm us."

"Humpf!" snorts Grimpen. "What are you using?"

"An Anti-Magic Shell. I'm afraid your staff will cease to function for a short period of time."

"We'll have light enough, believe me!" Grimpen predicts ominously.

Suddenly Luben Warlock points his hand straight at you! Instinctively you duck. Beside you, Father Justin murmurs his chant. Filled with a horrible fascination, you watch as the meteors swarm across the room, one going to each corner. There is an explosion that nearly deafens you, and you are blinded by the brilliant orange light.

Miraculously, you remained untouched. You can't even feel the heat. Overcome with relief, you laugh out loud and are joined immediately by Eric and the Blue Lady. Even your brother manages a grim smile.

When the smoke and flames clear, you look for Luben Warlock. He's gone!

"We'll meet later. You're not through with me yet . . ." you hear his voice echo through the chamber.

Please turn to page 116.

To your amazement, as you approach the west door, it swings wide open!

"That's strange! Let me go in first," Eric says, frowning and drawing his sword.

You pull out your knife and follow. As Eric steps through the door, a bright light streams from the room. Eric cries out and staggers back out of the room, bumping into you. You manage to peer around him, and as the light fades, you glimpse something.

"I couldn't see a thing!" Eric says, rubbing his eyes. "That light seemed to explode right in front of me!"

"I saw a book on a wooden table!" you cry.

"What does it look like?" Grimpen asks eagerly.

"It's red," you tell the wizard, "and I think it has golden runes on the cover."

"My master's spellbook!" Grimpen shouts, starting toward the room. "Let me pass, Gregor!" the wizard exclaims.

"Stop him—any way you can!" Eric shouts. "The book might be black magic!"

"No, Gregor!" Father Justin pleads. "The company must remain true to each other!"

1) If you agree with Eric, stop the wizard by knocking him down with a punch to his jaw. Turn to page 17.

2) If you agree with Father Justin, then simply step aside and let the wizard go into the west room. Turn to page 85.

"You're nothing but a coward!" you scream at your brother. "You let my mother die, and now we're all going to die because of you!"

"You're right," Lord Bloodstone mumbles. He slumps against the wall, his spirit shattered. "I'm sorry, Gregor. I'm sorry. . . ."

A chilling numbness spreads over you, but it isn't from the touch of the wraith. Not yet.

It is the chill that comes from not loving, not caring about anybody. And you realize—too late—that this is why you will fail in your quest. If you had given your brother the love and faith he needed, he would have found the courage to save you.

"It's not your fault!" you cry. "It's I who am sorry!"

"I'm not," whispers the wraith as its hand reaches out for you.

THE END

"I don't think I have any right to try to stop Grimpen," you say. "If he chooses evil, then it must be his own decision."

The wizard studies you a moment, his gray eyebrows drawn close together. You have the feeling he is trying to make up his mind about something. At last he sighs. Reaching out, almost timidly, he pats your shoulder. "Well put, gypsy." The wizard smiles at you, and suddenly you are no longer afraid of him.

Grimpen must have seen terrible things here when he was young, you think. No wonder he acts so detestable sometimes. Maybe he's just as frightened as you are.

"I'll come with you if you like," you offer.

The wizard looks startled, then nods and enters the room. You follow hesitantly, curious to see what is there.

The book rests on a plain wooden table. It's bound in red leather, with golden runes on the cover and spine.

"This is it!" the wizard breathes. "My master's spellbook! With this, I have a chance to defeat the wizard who murdered my master, Ian Whitestone!"

"I didn't know you were his apprentice," the Blue Lady says as she enters the room. "He was one of the very finest of the good wizards."

"Yes . . . and now my years of study will finally pay off!" Grimpen declares.

Softly he begins to murmur ancient words. Closing his eyes, he moves his hands in the air slowly, deliberately. Then he walks over and picks up the spellbook. He strokes the binding lovingly, then leafs through the brittle parchment pages.

"Look!" he cries suddenly. "Here's the spell to release the door to the Room of the Silver Moon and Stars! Unfortunately it won't open it. Someone still has to push it open."

"Great!" you cry. "Now maybe we can get somewhere."

1) If you have been to the east room and acquired what you need there, you know what to do next and may turn to page 112.

2) If you want to try to get past the golem using the magic spellbook alone, turn to page 99.

3) If you think you should go to the east room now, turn to page 93.

"I agree with Eric," you say stoutly. "I wouldn't go on a quest for a stale piece of bread with that washed-up wizard."

"Ha-ha," Eric laughs heartily. "Well put, Gregor!"

"Washed-up wizard, is it?" Grimpen Seventhson hisses. "We'll see about that!" The wizard raises his staff. Eric draws his sword.

"Stop this madness!" Father Justin cries, then begins to chant in a monotone voice. You cannot understand the words, yet you can feel peace descend upon the company. Eric lowers his sword. The wizard remains frozen.

Suddenly the cleric's voice fails. "I—I can't continue," Father Justin cries. "The evil in this room is too strong! We're letting the curse work on us!"

"I thought you said the evil couldn't come out!" You grab hold of Father Justin's robes. "What's happening?"

Suddenly the room is filled with the sound of wicked laughter, followed by an evil voice: "The evil never came out because it was never threatened." You stare around in horror.

"It's Luben Warlock!" The wizard's beard bristles.

"Yes, Seventhson. And now my victory is complete. You are all under my power. There is no hope for you. You cannot overcome me now!"

Father Justin grabs you by the shoulder. "The evil in this room is too powerful to fight! Run, Gregor!"

"I—I can't leave you," you cry.

Father Justin shoves you with a strength you would not have guessed he had. "Run!" he screams.

You take a few hesitant steps, then a bolt of lightning sizzles through the room. It flashes around the spellbound wizard's staff and streaks out toward Eric. Eric deflects the bolt with his sword, but the force knocks him to the ground.

Father Justin leaps forward, throwing himself over Eric's motionless body. The next bolt of lightning strikes the cleric, who collapses, his robes afire.

Horrified, you watch long enough to see your brother grab Eric's sword and rush toward the wizard.

Turning in terror, you flee. Behind you, there is another bright flash, then a dreadful clap of thunder. Flames leap from the room as the ceiling crashes in.

As you run through the hallway, it seems as if the Manor itself is collapsing around you. As you choke in the smoke and collapse against the door, the last thing you see is the bloodstone ring on your finger. And the last voice you hear is the wild, maniacal laughter of Luben Warlock.

THE END

"Take the chalice, Father," you urge. "You can always come back for the water if we need it, but the wererats might find some way to steal the chalice."

"You're right," Father Justin says, nodding. "The water will be here forever."

"This way!" Eric leads the group through another door that faces south. "Hurry! The wererats are getting close!"

You hurry down another winding corridor that slopes downhill. Occasionally you slip on the damp floor. Rounding a bend, you bump into Eric, who has come to a sudden halt.

"Whoa!" he exclaims. Looking past his shoulder, you see a heavy wooden door. Eric tries the latch, but it's fastened.

"I can pick the lock," you say eagerly, anxious for a chance to help.

"Wait," Eric cautions. He puts his head to the door, and his face grows serious.

"What is it?" Father Justin asks.

Now you hear it, too. Snarling sounds from beyond the door grow louder by the minute. Soon the noise echoes through the corridor. Suddenly you hear the wererat feet behind you stop, then retreat.

"Whatever it is, it scared off the wererats," Eric observes.

"Not for long," Grimpen sniffs. "Let the gypsy open the door."

The snarling sounds from beyond the door have grown softer. "Maybe they're gone." You look at Eric. "I don't hear them anymore."

"Then the wererats will be returning. Open the door, Gregor. Then stand aside. I'll enter first," Eric says.

You study the lock by the light of the wizard's staff, then select a thin, delicate piece of wire from your belt. Inserting the wire into the lock, you hold your breath and wiggle it gently. There is a loud click, and the door begins to swing open.

Eric shoves you aside and steps in, his sword gleaming in the wizard's magic light. You wait by the door, peering into the darkness, seeing only the vague outline of the fighter's body. Suddenly there is a crash, and you hear Eric yell fiercely, "Kobolds! It's a trap!" You grab your knife in alarm.

"Help him!" Father Justin orders. Your brother has turned deathly pale, but he takes a deep breath, then plunges into the room with you at his heels. The wizard, behind you, lights the room with his staff. By its glowing light, you see a terrible sight.

Two doglike creatures have wrestled Eric to the ground. The fighter's sword lies on the floor, out of his reach. He struggles with one of the kobolds, who raises a spear.

The wizard grabs the creature from behind, muttering in a strange language. The kobold screams as a fiery bolt surges through its body. The creature slumps, lifeless, to the floor, but not before it has driven its spear through Eric's chest. The other kobold flees through the door, howling an alarm.

"Eric!" Father Justin runs to the dying warrior. "I must return for the Holy Water!"

"The wererats are there by now," your brother says. "You'll never make it."

"That kobold was only a guard. More will be along," Grimpen says. "I have a spell or two left, but that won't hold them off for long. We're trapped!"

"Maybe the chalice has some sort of healing power," you cry.

Father Justin lifts the chalice into the air, chanting a prayer. Then he stops. You stare in horror as the chalice's gold turns to an ugly green, then the jewels crack and fall to the ground. "It's a fake!" Father Justin cries. He hurls the useless chalice into a corner of the room in frustration.

"Forgive me, Eric!" he weeps, kneeling beside the stricken adventurer.

"No talk of forgiveness is necessary between us," the fighter murmurs. "Die bravely, my friends!"

The snarling grows louder. It sounds like hundreds of kobolds coming at you from one direction. A pack of fierce wererats approach from the other. There is no way out.

"Are you afraid?" you ask your brother softly.

"No—not any more." He puts his arm around you and holds you close as snarling creatures burst into the room from both sides.

THE END

You approach the east door warily. To your amazement, it swings open as you approach it!

"I don't like the looks of that at all," Father Justin mutters.

As you start to enter the room, Eric jumps in front of you. "Hold it, Gregor! You're likely to run into another iron golem—or worse—if you're not careful."

"You're right, Eric." You stop to listen but hear nothing.

Eric enters first, his weapon drawn. "Light, wizard!" you hear him call out. Grimpen Seventhson shines the light from his staff into the room. "Nothing!" Eric says, puzzled.

You look into the room. It's empty, except for an old wooden chest next to one wall. The chest is intricately carved, with elaborate designs decorating its smooth finish.

"Whatever we're looking for must be in that box," your brother says.

"That sounds too easy," Eric says with a frown. "I don't trust it. Gregor, I assume Hugo taught you how to open boxes that are booby-trapped. It's up to you. If you want to take the risk, go ahead and open it. Otherwise I say we leave it alone."

1) If you decide to risk opening the box, turn to page 27.

2) If you prefer to leave the box alone, turn to page 47.

"I will not steal—not for you or for anybody!" you say through clenched teeth.

"Oh, you won't, eh?" Hugo snarls, raising one huge fist. "Maybe a little bloodletting will clear your head!"

Hugo swings mightily, but you duck quickly and avoid the blow. Hugo loses his balance and falls down into the filth in the alley. You recognize your chance to escape! You try to dash around Hugo, but the large gypsy leaps to his feet.

Suddenly you see a flash of steel. A knife gleams in Hugo's hand. He lunges at you, but you are more agile than the older man and leap backward. The knife blade whistles past your head, slashing your shirt. As Hugo recovers his balance, you take to your heels, racing down the narrow side street.

"This time you've gone too far, Gregor!" Hugo snarls. "This time I'll cut your tongue out!" You hear the sound of his boots pounding after you.

You dash back into the marketplace, pushing your way through the crowd, with Hugo close behind. You can hear him uttering oaths in the gypsy tongue.

You are forced to slow down as the crowd thickens. Glancing back, you see Hugo, the knife gleaming in his hand. You look at the grim, uncaring faces around you—each person concerned only with himself. You know that no one will lift a hand to help you.

Your heart races, and you begin to gasp for

air. Shoving and pushing, you claw your way through the pressing bodies. Suddenly you spot a small opening in the crowd! You dive down a side street, only to find an overturned cart blocking your path! You hear Hugo laugh evilly.

"Where is the old woman when you need her most, eh, Gregor? You are cornered, my friend!"

Frantically you search for a way out. All at once, without noticing where it came from, you see a knife appear on the ground at your feet. A cleric dressed in brown robes and wearing a holy amulet around his neck stands beside the knife. You notice at a glance that the cleric is crippled. He stands crookedly, resting his weight on his one good leg.

"Are you in trouble, my son?" the cleric asks. "May I help you?"

The cleric looks at you with strange, penetrating eyes. He seems to be offering you a choice. You can make a grab for the knife and face Hugo or seek the cleric's protection.

1) If you want to reach for the knife, turn to page 18.

2) If you decide to ask the cleric for help, turn to page 34.

"Let's fight the golem and get it over with," you say, pulling out your knife.

"Good for you, Gregor!" Eric says, drawing his sword. "With Lord Bloodstone's magic sword and your enchanted knife, we've got a fighting chance. Are we ready?"

You nod grimly. Eric leads the way down the corridor. Father Justin, Grimpen Seventhson, and the Blue Lady stay back near the door. You hear Father Justin's voice rising in a chant that renews your courage.

The golem advances toward you, its thundering footfalls shaking the earth. Your heart beats faster as it nears, and you begin to think you made a bad suggestion. How can you ever hope to defeat this metal giant?

"Aim for the legs!" Eric rushes forward, swinging his sword at the creature's calf muscles. His sword clangs against the golem, like someone hitting a huge gong. Eric cries out in pain and staggers backward.

"Eric!" you cry, starting toward him.

"Look!" he gasps. "My sword didn't even make a dent in that thing!"

"Puny human!" the golem thunders. "I will squash you like a grape!" You watch in horror as it reaches down and picks up Eric in one huge hand. The fighter struggles in vain but can't escape the creature's iron grip.

"Use your magic weapons!" Eric screams. "Hurry! It's crushing me!"

Screaming, you rush forward and sink your magic blade into the golem's toe. It howls and

jerks its foot back quickly, sending you flying.

"I injured it," you cry, "but I've lost my knife!" You stare hopelessly at your knife, still stuck in the golem's foot, then duck as the golem aims a vicious kick at you.

Eric screams in agony as the golem tightens its grip on the fighter. You flatten yourself against the wall in terror.

"Let's see what the magic sword will do!" your brother shouts. He swings the magic Sword of Valor, and the enchanted blade bites deeply into the golem's leg. The golem howls in rage but continues to advance.

"Use your magic!" you hear the Blue Lady call to the wizard. Grimpen starts to mutter strange words, but they are immediately drowned out by the golem's angry roar.

"No magic!" it rumbles. As you watch in horror, the creature hurls Eric through the air. His body slams into the Blue Lady and the wizard, knocking them both to the floor. You try to crawl to them, but one look tells you that they are all unconscious, perhaps dead.

"Help! Gregor!" you hear your brother yell. Frantically you turn back, only to see the golem stomp its huge foot down on Bloodstone's helpless form. You close your eyes as the golem lifts its other foot just above you. As it descends, you realize that for you, like the others in your party, this is . . .

THE END

"Now that we've got the magic spellbook," you say excitedly, "I say we use it to get past the golem!"

"Let's go!" Eric says decisively.

Carefully you open the north door. At the far end of the corridor, the iron golem stirs.

"I am the Guardian!" it booms. "Who goes there?"

"Let us pass in peace, golem," Eric calls.

"None may pass," the golem intones. "Death to those who try to pass!"

"All right, wizard!" Eric growls. "Do your stuff!"

The wizard leafs frantically through the book. "I'm going to conjure up a rust monster!" he announces. Quickly he searches his pouches and drags out a small piece of candle and a tiny bag. Then he begins to read the words of the spell and make the prescribed hand motions.

The iron golem starts down the hall toward you.

"Hurry!" Eric urges, glaring at the wizard.

"I've never cast this spell before!" Grimpen snaps. "Don't rush me! . . . There!" he says triumphantly.

Nothing happens.

"WHERE?" Eric shouts frantically.

"I summoned a rust monster," the wizard explains, frowning. "I wonder what could have happened. . . . Oh, my!"

You look up to see the golem halfway down the corridor. You begin inching back toward the door, your brother following, stumbling over his feet.

"I—I misjudged the distance somehow," the wizard says apologetically, stroking his beard. "The rust monster is indeed here. Unfortunately it is shut up inside the Room of the Silver Moon and Stars."

"What do we do now?" Father Justin asks excitedly.

"We either fight or go back," Eric says grimly.

"We must have whatever is in that east room!" you cry. "We've got to try to get in there!"

1) If you decide to fight the golem, turn to page 96.

2) If you want to go back to explore the east room, turn to page 93.

3) If you think you should take the spellbook and leave, turn to page 140.

"What do you think, wizard?" you ask. "You've been here before."

"We should go west," Grimpen Seventhson announces.

"West?" Eric shouts. "There are wererats down there! You can hear them!"

"But the boy is right. I AM the only one who has been here before," the wizard snarls, his beard quivering with anger. "And I say we go west."

"It's some kind of a trap," Eric argues.

"Perhaps," Father Justin says mildly. "But it also may lead to something very valuable. We'll have to fight the wererats sooner or later, Eric."

"Very well," the warrior sighs. "I can see I'm outvoted. We go west."

Drawing his sword, he steps into the corridor. You follow behind, your golden knife gleaming in your hand. Behind you, you can hear your brother's shallow breathing. Father Justin and the wizard bring up the rear. The wizard holds his staff high, casting light down the corridor.

The passageway is filthy, full of garbage, old bits of rusted armor, and occasionally the body of some dead animal. The smell chokes you. The wererat voices grow louder.

You hear one snarl, "I tell you I heard a noise!"

"And I tell you it was merely the growling of your stomach waking you up."

"Very funny, garbage-breath," the other

voice snarls. "There! I smell humans! That noise I heard could be our dinner."

More wererat voices join in, followed by the sound of slobbering laughter. Eric, creeping softly ahead of you, raises his hand. You stop.

"There're four of them," he whispers.

"Four!" Lord Bloodstone turns deathly pale. "Let's go back."

1) "We can fight four," you say stoutly. If you want to fight the four wererats, turn to page 58.

2) "I don't think we can handle that many," you say cautiously. "Let's go back to the Room of the Four Winds and try a different direction." If you want to go back, turn to page 23 and make another choice.

"I thank you, Father," you say, backing away. "Thank you for saving my life, and for this knife, and—"

"I did not give you the knife," the cleric protests.

"Then you won't mind if I sell it," you say. "I could probably get enough to live on for a year." While you speak, you continue to back away.

"But where will you go? What will you do?" The cleric appears concerned—or is he just disappointed that his prey is escaping?

You turn and set off at a run, deciding that you don't like this man's questions—or his answers, either, for that matter! As you run, you hear him calling after you. Crippled as he is, you know he can never catch you, so you ignore his cries. You just hope he doesn't cast a spell on you.

"There! I've escaped!" you think finally, when you can no longer hear him.

Entering a tavern that looks slightly less dirty than the rest, you pull out your deck of tarot cards.

"Have your fortunes told, gentlemen," you announce from the door. "The cost is just one small silver piece. And say, is anyone interested in buying a knife?"

THE END

"I'm going instead," you cry, and before anyone can stop you, you dash into the room.

A terrifying figure rises before you as you run toward the suspended sword. The figure is even blacker than the very darkness around you, but it is surrounded by a mysterious, chilling light. As it floats toward you, its eyes glitter and its hollow voice rings in your head.

"Living man! I hate your warm, living flesh. Now you will feel my cold and join me in the endless nightmare of undeath!"

"It's a wraith!" you hear Eric gasp. "Use your magic knife, Gregor!"

But the awful undead shadow fills you with such horror that you cannot move. The wraith comes closer and closer, intent on draining your life energy.

"Turn it, Father!" Eric cries.

"I—I can't!" Father Justin shouts back frantically. "Something is blocking me from going into the room—some sort of evil spell!"

"Help him, someone—anyone!" you hear your brother's voice shout.

"I'm going to try for the sword," Eric answers. "It's made of silver. It can kill the wraith." Eric runs into the room, and the wraith turns its malevolent glance toward him.

"Another warm, living being!" its horrible voice gloats. It floats forward and lays one chilling hand on Eric's shoulder. Eric cries out in anguish and falls to the ground, clutching his shoulder.

"You will be mine later!" the wraith says to Eric, then turns back to you, stretching out its cold hand.

You stare beseechingly at Lord Bloodstone. "Brother!" you cry. "Help me!" You glance at Lord Bloodstone's pale, trembling body and wonder if he can gather the considerable courage necessary to save you.

1) If you have faith in your brother, then call out to him to help you one more time. Turn to page 128.

2) If you are certain your brother is a coward and the situation is hopeless, turn to page 84.

"I think we should take the Holy Water," you say. "We'll need it if someone gets hurt. The chalice may be a holy symbol, but it's worthless to us. The wererats won't steal it if they haven't taken it before now."

"You're right, Gregor," Father Justin sighs. "The Holy Water could prove very useful to us. We may not be able to get back here again." Sighing, he stands up and lovingly replaces the Holy Chalice on the altar.

As he does so, something strange happens. The chalice's gleaming gold changes to an ugly green. The jewels fall from their mountings and shatter like worthless glass. Father Justin backs away, staring at the chalice in astonishment.

"It was a fake!" he breathes. Then he shudders. "Imagine what might have happened if I had taken it!"

"That must be why the wererats haven't bothered with it all these years," Eric says. "It was a cunning trap to deter any cleric from removing the truly valuable thing from this room—the Holy Water."

"This is all very interesting," the wizard says, "but speaking of wererats . . ."

"Yes." Father Justin nods, limping quickly to the fountain. "We must move along." He fills his water bag with the pure water, seals it carefully, and slings it over his shoulder, bending beneath the weight.

Eric leads the group through a door and down another corridor to the south. It slopes downhill gradually, twisting and bending until you have lost all sense of direction.

Traveling along the slick, slimy corridor, being careful to watch your footing, you round a bend and bump into Eric. Startled, you look up. Ahead of you is a closed wooden door. Eric begins to push on it gently. It starts to swing open with ease.

"Wait!" you command. "Hugo always said to beware unlocked doors. This could be a trap!"

"Well, if Hugo were here, we could send him in to find out, couldn't we?" the wizard says sarcastically.

"I can find out if there are any traps," you say, glancing at Eric, who nods.

Reaching into your belt, you draw out a copper coin. Stepping close to the door, you push it open the rest of the way slowly. Then you toss the coin into the darkness beyond. The coin strikes the stone floor with a loud ringing sound.

Immediately a snarling voice yells something in a strange language. You hear the sound of running feet as a creature rushes to investigate.

"Kobolds!" Eric says quickly. "But only two. Probably guards. We mustn't let them raise the alarm!"

Eric dashes through the door, his sword drawn. You watch as he engages the creatures in fierce combat. Soon Eric begins to fall back as the kobolds press their advantage. You know Eric can never defeat two of them. You look at your brother anxiously.

"We've got to help him fight!" you cry.

Bloodstone shakes his head. "I—I can't, Gregor," he pleads. "Don't ask me!"

"Very well," you say angrily. Drawing your magic knife, you leap into the room. One of the kobolds turns to face you. As it swings at you with its ax, you dodge backward.

Suddenly the knife in your hand seems to pull you forward. As the kobold tries to recover its balance from the swing, your knife plunges through its thick hide, and it falls with a faint gurgle.

You glance up just in time to see the other kobold drive a spear into Eric's chest! The fighter falls to the ground. You scream and run at the kobold. Intent upon its victim, it doesn't see you until your knife is in its back. It falls forward, lifeless, across Eric's body. Kicking the dead kobold off your friend, you kneel, ignoring the sound of more kobolds in the corridor.

"Father!" you shout. The cleric is beside you in moments.

"I am here, Gregor," he says as he takes the bag of Holy Water from his shoulder. Murmuring a prayer, he sprinkles the water over the wound and over Eric's face. Within seconds, the spear shaft vanishes as if it had never existed. The wound is gone!

Father Justin gasps. The Holy Water is gone, too! He stares at his empty hands, where the water bag had been only moments earlier.

"Thank you, Father," Eric mumbles, grinning at the sight of your shocked face. "Cheer up, Gregor. I'm not dead yet."

"Only a matter of time," Grimpen says, "now that we've lost our healing water." He holds his light up. You see an exit to the north—the way you came—one to the east, and another to the south. You hear wererats coming from the north and kobolds from the east. You hear nothing from the south.

"Close the doors on the north and the east," Eric orders, moving quickly. "Wizard, can you put a spell on the doors?"

"I can," Grimpen replies thoughtfully, "but I must have time. You'll have to hold them shut until I'm ready."

"Very well. Gregor, you and Lord Bloodstone hold that door. I'll take this one."

Both you and your brother lean against the door with all your strength. Soon you feel pressure on the other side.

Eric leans against his door and pushes it shut just as the kobolds appear. You hear them trying to smash it down.

Father Justin peers down the southern corridor, looking for danger. The wizard stands in the center of the room, leaning on his staff, apparently doing nothing.

"Hurry, confound you!" Eric shouts.

Grimpen begins making delicate motions in the air, pointing first to your door. Then he starts to sing in a high-pitched voice. The song's weird strains make the hair rise on the back of your neck. Lord Bloodstone shudders, and Father Justin holds his amulet close.

"Push hard, lads!" you hear a voice yell from the other side of the door. You feel the door begin to open, then it slams shut so suddenly it pulls you off your feet as the wizard casts his Hold Door Spell.

Howls of rage on the other side drown out the wizard's voice. Now he turns to face Eric's door. You see Eric straighten up, sighing with relief. The kobolds continue to hammer on it, but it will not budge.

"It's still clear to the south," Father Justin calls.

Once more Eric leads and you and the others follow. This time the corridor is flat and dry, making walking easier. You feel a warm, perfumed breeze waft through the corridor as soon as you leave the other room behind. Slowly you become aware of a blue light glowing ahead of you, growing brighter and brighter as you go along.

Your spirits begin to lift. The entire company moves faster, drawn toward the beautiful, enchanting light. Suddenly the corridor widens into a huge room. Blue light wells up from an object in the room's center. It's so bright that at first you must shield your eyes.

"Welcome to the Tomb of the Blue Lady," whispers a soft voice.

Please turn to page 133.

"I've got an idea," you say as you all gather outside the north door. "I can put on my cloak and sneak past the iron golem. The wizard can use his spell to release the door, and I can open it."

"It's worth a try," Eric says. "Go ahead, Gregor. Remember, though," he warns, "if the cloak fails, you'll be at the mercy of the golem."

"I'll be all right," you say with a grin.

"Good luck, Gregor." Your brother fastens the cloak around your shoulders. Then he blinks in astonishment, and you know you are now invisible. "I'll never get used to that!" he mutters.

Carefully you push open the north door.

"I am the Guardian!" the golem's voice rings through the hall. "Who goes there?"

Slowly you creep down the hall, coming closer and closer to the fearsome creature. The golem peers at the north door, looking puzzled.

"I am the Guardian!" it repeats angrily. "Who goes there?"

You hear the wizard's voice speaking very softly. Looking ahead past the golem, you see the door to the Room of the Silver Moon and Stars begin to glow faintly.

The golem starts crashing down the hallway toward you, its eyes on the open north door.

"I am the Guardian! I know you are there!" it booms. "Come no farther, on peril of your life!"

You see the iron golem coming closer and

closer as you creep down the hall. Suddenly it is right beside you! Hardly daring to breathe, you flatten yourself against the wall, hoping the cloak is working. Finally the golem thunders past.

"I am the Guardian!" it repeats, enraged.

Taking a deep breath, you run the remaining distance down the corridor until you stand before the door.

"You should be able to open it now!" the wizard shouts. "Pull hard, Gregor!"

You grab the ornate silver handle and tug mightily. The door barely moves. Using all your strength, you pull once more. Then you hear a sound like a heavy weight shifting, and you realize that the golem is turning around!

"I cannot see you, thief," it booms, "but I will crush you anyway!"

Desperately you continue to tug at the door. The wizard shouts a word of command, and suddenly the door flies open, knocking you on your back on the floor. Scrambling to your feet, you dash into the room.

There, standing right before you, is the most horrible monster you have ever seen! About seven feet tall, it's shaped like a giant rodent with a long scaly tail. It has no head, but two antennae protrude out from beneath its beady little eyes, located at the front end of its hideous, plate-mail body. It moves on four large feet.

You are caught between the iron golem and this—this thing! The monster looks up eagerly

and growls in excitement, then gallops straight toward you! You panic, then stare in wonder as the monster rushes past you out into the corridor.

"Of course!" you breathe, leaning limply against a wall. "It couldn't see me! I wonder what it was."

"A rust monster!" Eric shouts as he sees the creature emerge from the room.

Rushing to the door, you watch as the rust monster attacks the iron golem. As its antennae make contact with the golem, the creature immediately begins to rust wherever contact was made. The rust monster growls fiercely and renews its attack. Howling in pain, the golem tries to bash the rust monster with its sword, but its weapon also turns to rust.

While the two are fighting, Eric leads the rest of the group down the corridor at a run. The two monsters, engaged in a life-and-death struggle, do not seem to notice them.

Breathless, the group rushes into the Room of the Silver Moon and Stars and Eric slams the door shut.

"Well," he says, "we're here!"

"And you're very welcome, too," intones a voice.

Turning, you see Luben Warlock!

Please turn to page 37.

"Where—where is he?" you stammer.

"Come, we have little time to lose!" The Blue Lady starts through the smoke, heading for the hole in the wall. "Now that he is free," she says, "he will stop at nothing to keep us from our goal."

You stare around nervously, imagining the sorcerer's evil presence everywhere.

The Blue Lady notices your tenseness. "Don't worry. He won't face us here. He is waiting for us at the end."

"Where is that?" you ask with a shiver.

"Where we're going now—the Hall of Wizards. That is the final battleground, where we will put an end to the curse."

You sigh and walk through the opening in the wall. It leads south, into a narrow, dark corridor. At first you see nothing, but before long, the wizard's staff begins to glimmer faintly as the Anti-Magic Shell wears off. There are no signs of living creatures having been here for years. A thick layer of dust covers the floor.

"No wererats, at least," you point out.

"That won't stop them from coming, now that the enchantment is lifted," Eric says.

"I'm afraid you're right," the Blue Lady says, nodding. "We haven't much time."

Suddenly she stops and points straight ahead. You see two huge iron double doors, with strange symbols covering them. You are surprised to see them standing open. You're grateful for that until Eric shakes his head.

"As evil an invitation as I've ever seen!"

"We have no choice but to accept it," the Blue Lady says. "In one of these rooms, we must face Luben Warlock in the final confrontation to put an end to the curse."

"Is this the place?" Father Justin asks. He starts to rush in, but Eric stops him.

"Wait, Father!" he counsels. "A fighter should be first to go into the unknown." Then he remembers that he has surrendered his weapons and frowns. "Although I'm not much of a fighter anymore."

"Enter, Eric," the Blue Lady says softly.

Eric looks at her, then, moving cautiously, he steps through the door and into the shadows beyond. You hear him gasp.

"What is it?" Father Justin calls out.

Eric reappears in the doorway, his weapons and shield in his hands. The Blue Lady smiles. "You will need them before we are finished, brave warrior."

"It's empty," he says. "You may enter."

You walk through the door and your brother follows. Suddenly Bloodstone cries out. Turning, you see him clutching the Sword of Valor. As Father Justin walks through the door, the Holy Water appears in his hands. He gasps and nearly drops it in astonishment.

You see a room much like the Room of the Four Winds. There are four walls and four doors, leading north, south, east, and west. "Look!" you cry. "Each door is different."

Each silver door has a different set of

strange symbols traced on it. The door to the north shows a full moon with seven stars above it. The door to the east also has a moon and seven stars, but a cloud partially conceals the moon. The door to the west shows the earth's shadow eclipsing the moon, with the seven stars absent. The door to the south—the one you entered—has no moon at all. The seven stars shine alone in the sky.

"The fabled Hall of Wizards!" says the Blue Lady. "Through the door to the north is the Room of the Silver Moon and Stars. That is where we must go to end the curse."

"What are we waiting for?" you ask, heading for the door. Grimpen claps his hand on your shoulder and brings you to a sudden stop.

"Not so fast!" he snaps. "You can be sure something guards that door!"

"I'm afraid he's right," the Blue Lady says. "There IS a guardian at the door. But there is also a way to defeat him hidden in one of these other rooms."

"No doubt there will be traps in all the rooms," Eric says. "I say we try to fight whatever creature guards that door."

"I think we should investigate the other rooms," says Grimpen.

"You just want to find that spellbook!" Eric says accusingly.

"We might need it before we're through!"

"Let's vote," says Father Justin. "Eric?"

"I say we fight the guardian and get it over with. I vote north."

"Seventhson?"

"West. The moon is in eclipse, which suggests good eclipsing evil."

"Or vice versa," Eric growls.

"Lord Bloodstone?"

"I suggest we go back south," your brother says, smiling wanly. "Maybe we can escape before the wererats and kobolds discover the enchantment has been removed."

"And you, Father?" Eric asks.

"I say we go east. The cloud over the moon may mean something is hidden there."

"Blue Lady?" Eric continues.

"I take no part in this," she replies. "It is your quest, and you must decide."

All turn to look at you.

"Your vote decides, Gregor," Eric says.

You swallow hard and look once again at the four doors, your mind racing.

1) If you vote to head north and fight the unknown guardian, turn to page 60.

2) If you elect to go south and try to get out of here, turn to page 140.

3) If you choose to set out to the east and see if something is hidden there, turn to page 132.

4) Or if you vote to go west to see if good really does eclipse evil, turn to page 42.

You realize that for perhaps the first time in your life, you feel good about yourself. You just have to stay!

"I guess I'll stay and listen to what you have to say." You sit down once more.

A gust of chill wind blows through the room from the open door. The fire flickers once, then dies.

You see two men in the doorway. One is tall and slender, the other old and bent.

You note appreciatively the velvet and silk and lace the tall man is wearing. He is not much past thirty, with black hair, worn long, and curls falling to his shoulders. He is wrapped in an expensive full-length cloak. He is dressed entirely in black, with only the white lace at his throat and shirt cuffs providing relief. You decide he is a nobleman and wonder what he is doing in this foul tavern.

"So he came," Eric murmurs softly.

"And Grimpen Seventhson with him," Father Justin adds.

Eric shrugs. "What did you expect? I've never trusted that scheming wizard, though."

"Wizard!" you gulp, and the old man's bent head swings toward you. Black, gleaming eyes shine in the dim light. He is old, old beyond time itself. His long beard may have once been white but now is yellow with age. He seems harmless enough, but you note the shrewd, calculating gaze and the thin, unsmiling lips. An aura of power seems to radiate from his bent body.

As the two strange newcomers approach your table, men-at-arms take their places outside the tavern door. The nobleman stares down at all of you with a sneer on his lips.

"Lord Bloodstone." Father Justin rises and bows low. "We have much to discuss."

Lord Bloodstone sits in a chair the innkeeper provides. You stare at the tall figure curiously. He is pale, with deep circles beneath his eyes. One hand shakes almost imperceptibly, and you recognize the unmistakable signs of a drunkard.

"Bring wine!" he orders the innkeeper. "An evil place, the Ten Swords. But the wine is good . . . and so is my credit."

The innkeeper thumps the dusty bottle down on the table. Ignoring the flagon beside it, Lord Bloodstone picks up the bottle. "To the quest!" he says bitterly and drinks deeply.

All the while, the wizard has remained standing behind Lord Bloodstone.

"There is no chair for you, Seventhson," Eric says suddenly, scowling.

The wizard cackles and snaps his fingers. Unaided by human hand, a chair skitters across the floor to him. You gulp and glance at Eric, who appears unimpressed.

"My lord, you know why we are here," Father Justin begins.

"Oh, yes." Lord Bloodstone takes another deep drink of wine. "The council has ordered me to unbrick the catacombs. Fools!"

"The council reached its decision only after

months of study," Father Justin continues. "The curse is spreading, my lord! Surely you don't want the rest of the world to fall under its spell like this town!"

Lord Bloodstone shrugs. "I really couldn't care less," he replies negligently.

"It is out of your hands," Eric says coldly. "The White Council has ordered it."

"The White Council!" sneers the wizard. "That group of imbeciles need not concern you, my lord. Let us take leave."

"Still bitter, Grimpen Seventhson?" Eric says, glaring. "There was good reason why you were dismissed from the council!"

"Lies!" The wizard stands suddenly, his gray eyebrows bristling in anger.

"Please, gentlemen! We must not start our quest with an argument!" Father Justin begs.

"We must not start it at all," Lord Bloodstone mutters. "Death . . . nothing but death in the catacombs!"

"Death may indeed be what we face," Father Justin murmurs. "If so, that is in hands other than ours. Each of us goes in search of something dearer than life. I have been chosen by the council to rid the catacombs of the curse that dwells there and thus free the land from bondage."

"And what do you risk your life for, Eric, Prince of the Windswept Dunes?" Seventhson asks. "Yes, I recognized you under those rags."

"The White Council asked me to make the journey. I go to protect the company."

"And seek the Blue Lady?" the wizard asks with an evil laugh.

You see Eric grow pale in the darkness. "That is my own concern," he answers.

"And is the gypsy boy prepared to die in the Endless Catacombs?" Grimpen sniffs.

"I—I'm not prepared to die anywhere!" you stammer.

"The boy has his own reasons for going," Father Justin interrupts, "though he may not fully understand them yet."

"A gypsy?" Lord Bloodstone looks up for the first time, a flicker of interest in his dark eyes. Suddenly a grip like iron pins your wrist to the table. Startled, you stare in amazement at the lord, who holds you in his grasp. His eyes are fixed on your ring.

"You're—you're hurting me, my lord," you protest weakly.

"Where did you get that ring?" Bloodstone demands through trembling lips.

"He stole it," Grimpen says quickly.

"The ring is his, just as the matching ring is yours, my lord," Father Justin says, pointing. Now you see a ring identical to the one you wear on Lord Bloodstone's hand. "The boy was found twelve years ago near the Fanged Rocks, half-dead, beside the body of his mother. She had been killed by wererats. The ring hung around his neck on a golden chain."

"So she and my brother made it as far as the Fanged Rocks . . ." Lord Bloodstone whispers, his eyes half-closed.

"Brother!" you gasp. You try to pull away from him, but he only tightens his grip.

"Yes, it is true. You are my brother."

"Nonsense! This is merely a trick of the White Council," Grimpen Seventhson snarls.

"It's no trick," Eric interjects. "We knew nothing of the boy until today. Obviously higher forces are at work here."

"The forces of evil," Lord Bloodstone mutters, lifting his head, his dark, haunted eyes on you. "You are very much like her, boy." He shakes his head. "I was to have gone with them, you know—into the Endless Catacombs." Lord Bloodstone stares into his wine. "The castle was under attack. . . ."

"The Siege of Bloodstone," Eric says, nodding. "A bitter battle."

"My father fell among his men," Bloodstone continues, unhearing. "I was seventeen at the time. His last words were to order me to take my mother and younger brother into the catacombs. We were to hide there until reinforcements arrived from the king." His words end in a muffled choke.

"Brother!" you repeat, stunned.

"Hush," Father Justin counsels softly.

"I couldn't go through that terrible arch!" Lord Bloodstone goes on, not even noticing the interruption. "The stench of evil flowed from the darkness of the catacombs! The only reason my mother left my father's side was to protect my brother and me. She would have preferred to die beside him.

"She begged, pleaded, commanded! I couldn't force myself to move. The battle grew near. Finally my mother kissed me and told me to hide in a small niche in the wall, big enough for one. Then she took my brother by the hand and walked through the archway into the darkness of the catacombs. That was the last time I ever saw her."

You hear Father Justin whisper a prayer. Even Eric appears moved. You brush your hand across your eyes. The wizard does not seem to have been listening.

"I hid where she told me," Lord Bloodstone continues in a whisper, "and I escaped detection. None would go near that dreadful door. Finally the king's men arrived and I was rescued. I was now lord of this miserable city, and my first command was to brick up the entrance to the Endless Catacombs. My second command was to bring a flask of wine. I do not recall being sober since."

"Why did you have them brick up the entrance?" Eric asks. "According to the old legends, the evil can never come out."

"No, the evil does not come out, though the curse fills the land," Bloodstone says slowly, his blurry eyes staring at Eric. "I heard her calling me . . . calling for help. Finally her calls ceased, and all I heard were the sounds of the wererats. Nothing could have saved her! But night after night, long after I knew she was dead, I could still hear her voice, calling me from that evil place. That is why I bricked it up—to block out the sound. Only it didn't work! Still—night after night—I hear her calling to me. . . ." He gulps down the wine, then lays his head on his arms. You realize he has passed out.

"Quite a band of heroes, aren't we?" the wizard cackles as he strokes his beard, his rotten teeth gleaming. "A cowardly drunk, a gypsy waif, a lovesick prince, a crippled cleric, and a defrocked wizard."

You stand up suddenly. "I'm not going anywhere with any of you, especially this—this drunkard who calls me his brother! And as for this ring—"

"It is your birthright, Gregor," Father Justin interrupts sternly. "Deny it and you deny yourself. As for your brother, he deserves your pity and your help, not your hatred. If you come with us, there is a chance you might save him."

Undecided, you put your hand on the ring.

1) If you want to take the ring off, return it to your brother, and refuse to have anything more to do with this dangerous quest, turn to page 29.

2) But if you decide to wear the ring proudly, go on the quest, and make the name "Bloodstone" worthy of honor once more, turn to page 139.

"Please, brother!" you plead. "I know you're not a coward!" And as you say the words, you realize you really do believe them.

Even as you call out, the wraith sweeps closer. You try to ignore it, keeping your gaze on Lord Bloodstone. Finally he takes a deep breath and slips softly into the room.

You back away, intent on keeping the undead creature from seeing your brother. You think about your magic knife, but your arm seems paralyzed. It's all you can do to move your feet. A numbing coldness has spread throughout your entire body. The wraith laughs and stretches out its hand.

Suddenly Lord Bloodstone lunges and grabs the silver sword. There is a blinding flash of pure white light and a bloodcurdling scream. Then blessed warmth surrounds you, and your brother has you in his arms.

Father Justin rushes into the room, puts his hand on Eric's shoulder, and murmurs a prayer. You watch as the pain eases on the fighter's face and he rises to his feet.

"Thank you, Father," he says simply. "And thank you, Lord Bloodstone. The Sword of Valor has found a worthy master."

"I hear tramping feet," snaps the wizard, cocking his head. "Once the wererats find out the wraith is dead, they'll be after us!"

"There's a doorway to the south," Eric says quickly, pointing. "Let's go!"

Please turn to page 151.

"I'm smarter than these oafs," you think. "I don't need to fight!"

"Let's give him a thrashing!" one of the men growls, raising his hand to smack you across the face. You think quickly.

"Look there!" you yell, pointing at the man's hand. "What a wonder! Only twice in my entire life have I ever seen that mark!"

"What mark?" The man stops in midswing and stares at his hand curiously.

"Those lines on the Delta of Venus. I've seen such lines only twice before—both men were great lovers. The same is true of you, sir— correct? Don't the ladies gather outside your blacksmith shop just to watch you work?"

"Garn!" The man loosens his hold on you in astonishment. "How did you know that? And how did you know I was a blacksmith?"

You begin to relax. "It is written in your palm," you say mysteriously.

"What else do you see?" Eagerly the man shoves his dirty hand beneath your nose.

Relieved, you begin to trace the lines on the man's hand, predicting long life and many children. Finally he and his friends leave, eager to spread the tale.

Flushed and embarrassed, you return to the booth, half-ashamed of your performance.

"How did you know that man was a black-smith?" Eric asks, one eyebrow raised.

"It's an old gypsy trick," you reply, blushing. "A big part of fortune-telling is observing peo-ple closely. I could tell he was a blacksmith by the way he was dressed, the bulging muscles in his shoulders and neck, and the black soot ground into his hands."

"I see," Eric says, beginning to smile faintly. "Then what am I?"

Eric leans forward. You examine his clothing. It's worn and bears the stains of travel. He is muscular, confident, fearless. . . . You notice an air of nobility about him as well, though he obviously wants this kept secret, for his clothing is ragged.

"You are an adventurer," you answer, "in search of adventure."

"I might say the same of you, Gregor the gypsy." Eric laughs suddenly. "Will you join us? I have a feeling we will be able to use a quick mind such as yours after all. But our search will be a dangerous one."

"I—I don't know where you're going," you protest, "or what you're searching for."

"Each searches for his own reward," Father Justin replies evenly. "You, Gregor, will be searching for the answer you have sought all your life—your true identity. However, you may not find the answer you expect—or want. Have you the courage to find out?"

1) If you have the courage to accompany Father Justin and Eric in their search, turn to page 120.

2) But if you are content to continue leading a gypsy's life, turn to page 135.

"I don't want to face up to whatever's behind that north door yet," you say. "Let's investigate the east room. As Father Justin says, there may be something hidden there."

You walk over to the door and place your hand on the handle. There is a blinding flash as a jolt of electricity knocks you backward onto the floor.

Father Justin hurries over to where you sit and shakes you vigorously. "Are you all right, Gregor?" he asks.

"Y-Yes, I think so," you say after a moment to get your breath back. "What happened?"

"Apparently we can't get in there," Grimpen says. "Try the west door."

"YOU try the west door yourself!" you mutter as you pick yourself up.

The wizard approaches the west door, then reaches out with his staff. It stops about three inches from the handle. "A force field," he says.

"We have no choice but to go north," Eric says grimly.

"Oh, yes, we do," your brother states. "We can get out of here!" He walks over to the south door, but just as he reaches it, the door slams shut in his face!

"It looks like we go north," you say with a sigh.

Please turn to page 60.

Shadowy columns support a high ceiling. A sense of peace and beauty fills the room and your heart. You feel you never want to leave. As your eyes become accustomed to the light, you look into the center of the columns to see where the light comes from, and you gasp.

The strange blue light radiates from a crystal coffin standing on a raised dais in the center of the room. In the tomb lies the still figure of a lovely young woman, her eyes closed, her hands at her side. She does not seem to be breathing.

"The Blue Lady!" Eric murmurs softly. "I have found you at last!"

For a moment, Eric seems overcome. His head sinks into his hands. Then you watch as the fighter strides forward joyfully to be beside the woman he has loved for so long. But after only a few steps, he finds his way blocked by an invisible barrier.

"What's this?" he cries, seeming to beat his hands on empty air in frustration.

A soft, deep voice fills the chamber: "Welcome, you who have entered the Tomb of the Blue Lady. You have come here with a purpose. It may be good. It may be evil. I will help those who come here for a good cause. I will thwart those who come here for evil purposes. To prove your worth, you may enter the tomb only if you have two objects—Holy Water from the fountain and the Sword of Valor. These may be won only by the good and the valiant. All others will fail and meet their doom.

"If you have both of these objects, you may proceed to the next part of your quest. If you have only one of the magical objects, you must go back for the other. Return to the Room of the Four Winds and keep searching until you find the other magical object I have placed to help you."

Her voice falls silent.

1) If you have found both magical objects, you may continue on with your adventure. Turn to page 24.

2) If you still need to search for the other magical object, turn to page 74.

"Thank you, gentlemen," you say with a flourish, "but a gypsy's life is a good life. I won't give it up to go on a quest with a crippled cleric and a stern-faced ranger. I am not fond of danger. I prefer music and dancing, good food, and a warm place to sleep. As for knowing myself, I know I am a gypsy, and I desire to be nothing more."

Flipping your knife in the air, you catch it casually and put it back in your sash, then saunter from the Inn of the Ten Swords. Once outside, you breathe a sigh of relief.

That was just too strange! Running down the street, you decide to try to win back Hugo's favor by giving him your new knife, never once pausing to think that, for you, the adventure has come to an . . .

END

"I think we should try using magic first," you argue. "There's no way we can fight that thing and win, even with enchanted weapons."

"Oh, very well," the wizard grumbles. "But I warn you, if I expend all my energy, I may not have enough left to do what must be done in the room beyond."

"We'll just have to take that chance," Eric growls.

"Stand back, then!" the wizard barks, casting a baleful glance at Eric. He reaches into his pouch and pulls out a bit of fur and a small amber rod.

"Hurry!" you breathe. The golem is getting nearer. You can feel the ground tremble with each footfall.

Concentrating deeply, the wizard closes his eyes and begins reciting the spell. As the golem gets closer and closer, your brother grabs you and pulls you behind him.

Suddenly the wizard shouts something and points his hand. A jagged lightning bolt crackles from his fingers and strikes the golem. Electricity pulses through the creature's trembling body, and the golem roars and staggers backward.

"That did it!" Eric cries. "Blast it again, wizard!"

"I—I can't!" Grimpen gasps as his frail, weakened form begins to topple. You and your brother hurry to catch him before he hits the floor.

"It isn't stopping him! He's going to come at us again!" you yell.

"Blue Lady, can you help?" Father Justin asks hurriedly.

"I could teleport us out of here," she says, "but it will mean the end of the quest."

"Do it!" Eric orders. "Do it now, or we'll all be killed!"

Father Justin nods sadly. "Perhaps some-day we can come back," he says. "And then we will bring with us the means to defeat the Guardian."

"At least we're all still alive!" you cry. "That's something!"

"True enough." The Blue Lady looks at Eric. He puts his arm around her. Supporting the wizard, you huddle close together as the golem continues to recover and advance with an ever-quickening stride.

The Blue Lady speaks one word, and for you, the adventure comes to an . . .

END

"I can't believe all this is happening!" You feel dizzy. "This morning I was a gypsy trying to escape a beating, and now I'm a younger brother to the lord of this town, about to risk my life on some adventure I don't even understand!"

"You're a Bloodstone," Eric says with a shrug. "I'd say things are moving along fairly normally as far as your family is concerned. They were never noted for their good luck!"

"Well, maybe I'll just change that!" you reply grimly.

"Maybe you will at that," Father Justin says softly.

Please turn to page 49.

"Right now we're at a dead end. I think we should keep looking through the rest of the catacombs."

Ignoring the frowns on the faces of everyone except your brother, you walk back toward the door you came through before. Just as you reach it, however, it slams shut!

"That's the only way out!" Eric cries in alarm. He runs over and tries pulling at the door, but it doesn't budge. You see no sign of a handle. Frantically you search for a secret catch. The silver is smooth and solid.

"Trapped like rats!" says the wizard dourly. Trembling, you turn around.

Please turn to page 119 and choose another direction.

The corridor is littered with wererat garbage. It winds uphill at a slight angle, then drops back down and curves around to the north. Several openings lead off from it, and you occasionally stop to investigate these, but you hear wererat voices so you continue on. Soon you've passed the last of these openings, and the corridor continues on north, sloping steadily downhill. Suddenly Eric stops.

"Do you notice anything odd?" he asks.

You all look around.

"There are no traces of wererats anymore," Father Justin says at once.

"Right. And there haven't been any for the last several hundred feet. For some reason, the wererats don't come down this far."

"That's good," mumbles Lord Bloodstone.

"It may be—or it may not be," Eric says, frowning. "I'd guess there's something down here that even the wererats are afraid of. What do you say, wizard? Coming this way was your idea."

"I say we either go forward or backward," Grimpen snaps.

Eric glares at the wizard a moment, then shrugs and moves on ahead. You hurry to keep up with him.

"Ah-ha!" Eric exclaims, stopping suddenly.

You see only a blank wall. "A dead end?" you ask.

"More likely a secret door," Father Justin suggests.

"Of course!" you say, pleased at the chance

to show off your skills. "I can open it. Hugo showed me how."

Eric looks at you dubiously, then stands aside. You hurry up to the wall and run your hands across it.

"There's nothing there," Eric says after a moment.

"Wait," you breathe. Your skilled fingers have detected a tiny crack in the stone. Feeling slowly and carefully, you follow the crack until you feel certain it is a door. Then you think about all the methods for opening concealed doors that Hugo taught you. Getting down on your hands and knees, you examine the bottom of what appears to be a solid rock wall. Sure enough, you find a small piece of chipped stone. You pull the piece out and nearly fall over as the rock wall begins to slide open.

"Well done, Gregor!" Eric says warmly.

You stand and start to go through the door, but Father Justin's gasp halts you. "Don't! I sense a terrible presence in that room!" he warns.

Carefully Eric peers inside. "There's a sword in there!" he whispers in awe. "It's the most magnificent weapon I've ever seen!"

You poke your head beneath his arm to see. A sword, made of pure silver, hangs suspended in the middle of a pitch-dark room. It seems to be hanging in midair, with nothing supporting it. A single beam of white light, like a moonbeam, shines from a round globe on the ceiling, making the sword shimmer with silvery radiance.

"It's magnificent!" Lord Bloodstone gasps.

"The Sword of Valor!" gasps the wizard. "Only a person possessing true courage may claim it!"

"I'm going after it!" Eric declares.

"Don't!" Father Justin cries out, backing away from the room. "Turn back!"

"Why should Eric be the one who gets the sword?" you wonder. Perhaps you should try for it. Then you see Father Justin's face, wild with fear.

1) Do you want to make an attempt to get the Sword of Valor before Eric? If so, turn to page 104.

2) Or would you rather stand back and let Eric try for the sword? If this is what you decide, turn to page 70.

"I—I DO want a happy ending, if this isn't a trick! If you promise to remove the curse, and give everyone enough food to eat and decent places to live, and they don't get sick all the time. . . ."

"Done!" cries the sorcerer.

For a brief moment, you see your friends, their faces filled with dismay. But the moment disappears instantly as the Room of the Silver Moon and Stars dissolves around you.

Now you find yourself seated in Bloodstone Manor, obviously rebuilt and refurbished. Your brother, several pounds heavier, sits opposite you in a huge, overstuffed chair, laughing at some joke. You seem to have been here a long time. How long? You've lost track.

You laugh along with him in the sunshine streaming in through the window. You look outside and wave to a group of peasants, who wave back happily.

You spend the days that follow playing and singing and being merry. Everyone seems to be having a wonderful time. No one gets sick, no one dies, no one has to work.

Only gradually, dimly, do you realize that the world around Bloodstone Manor is neither growing nor changing. Nothing dies, but nothing is born, either.

And you think this might be wrong, but you are too busy having a good time to give the matter any serious consideration.

THE END

You watch as Eric thinks hard, his face drawn and stern. Then, in sudden decision, he unbuckles his sword belt and lays it at the foot of the crystal bier. He lays his shield down upon his sword, then kneels before the Blue Lady, his hands crossed on his chest.

"I have given you what you requested," he says simply. "My love will make up for what physical strength I now lack!"

Suddenly the blue light is quenched, plunging the chamber into darkness. Even the light from the wizard's staff goes out. Fearfully you reach out, and your brother's hand grasps yours reassuringly. "It was a trap!" you whisper hollowly.

"Wait," Eric says, his voice calm.

Slowly a figure emerges from the darkness. It glimmers in a soft blue light, which begins to glow brighter. Standing before you, you see the Blue Lady. She carries Eric's shield, and his sword belt is buckled around her slender waist. She approaches Eric and holds out her hand.

"Arise, Prince of the Windswept Dunes. Your love is indeed strong and will be rewarded. But now you must let me fight alone. No matter what happens, do not interfere. The foe I face I must face alone."

"Whom do you mean?" Eric demands.

The Blue Lady shakes her head, then fastens Eric's shield firmly to her left arm. With her right hand, she draws Eric's sword. The weapon looks much too big for her. Although there is strength and wisdom in her eyes, you wonder if she could possibly have matching strength in her body.

"Name the foe, fair lady, and let me fight him!" Eric cries.

"It's Luben Warlock!" Grimpen breathes.

The Blue Lady notices the wizard for the first time and smiles. "Why, well met, Grimpen Seventhson," she says. "You have changed over the years. You were just a boy when I saw you last. I must have slept a long time, judging by the length of your beard!"

"Luben Warlock!" Father Justin gasps.

Eric pales. "I will not allow you to face this danger alone!" he says decisively.

"You have given me all the help I require, my prince," the Blue Lady whispers to Eric. "Your great sacrifice and love will enable me to win out. Do not be afraid. I am not."

Eric bows his head as Father Justin begins to chant softly.

"The wizard can help!" you shout.

"No, not I," Grimpen Seventhson snarls. "I must conserve my strength. My spell-casting abilities have limits, you know."

"He could not help anyway," the Blue Lady replies. She reaches up and touches Eric gently on his cheek. Then, her blue dress shimmering around her slender body, she walks toward what appears to be a solid rock wall.

"Luben Warlock!" she calls loudly. You are amazed at the power in her voice. "It is time to face me at last!"

There is a loud creaking sound, and the wall begins to shiver. Finally it collapses into rubble, and a figure emerges.

You step back in horror. It seems as though all the evil in the world is embodied in the sorcerer's yellow cat's eyes.

Luben Warlock is young and very handsome, with black hair that curls around his temples and a strong, slender body. He moves with the fluid grace of a cat as he steps from the shattered wall as if he were stepping down from a throne. As you quake with fear, you are surprised to see him extend his hand to the Blue Lady and smile at her.

"You haven't changed," you hear him say, his voice rich and sweet. "And neither have I. Come with me, lovely lady, and we will rule the world!"

Hearing his sweet voice, you are convinced that the Blue Lady must agree to go with him. How could she possibly refuse? You see Eric watching in despair.

Suddenly the Blue Lady laughs, a laughter that sparkles like clear water and seems to break the spell that hangs over you.

"Luben Warlock," she replies firmly, "you know that I could rule the world without you, if I chose to do so. However, I want to be a part of the world, not control it. You won out last time, Luben, because I was not armed. Today I have weapons."

Now it is Luben's turn to laugh. Suddenly he is no longer handsome, though his appearance hasn't changed. All you see are the yellow cat's eyes and the gaping mouth.

"Weapons!" he says with a sneer. "You are a magic-user, Blue Lady. You can use neither shield nor sword to fight me."

"Of course not," the Blue Lady answers calmly. With a fluid sweep of her arms, she strikes the flat of the sword against the shield, and you hear a vibrant ringing sound. Then there is a flash of blue flame, and both the sword and shield vanish.

"Those were but the symbols of my weapons," she goes on, smiling. "My true weapons are love and faith. I hold love in the hand that held the blade. Love pierces the heart more surely than any sword. I am shielded by faith. This man and his friends believe in me, and their belief serves as my shield. All your weapons of evil have no power against me."

"We will see," Luben whispers evilly. You watch as he raises his hand and begins to speak soft, secret words. Slowly he traces a symbol in the air.

For the first time, you notice that Grimpen Seventhson appears alarmed. "We've got to get out of here!" he cries excitedly. "I know this spell! We'll all be killed!"

"I'm not leaving!" Eric declares, moving to stand beside the Blue Lady.

"Hurry!" Grimpen urges. "We must leave this lovesick idiot and escape while we can!"

You glance at the evil sorcerer, still speaking softly and tracing a pattern in the air. The

Blue Lady stands motionless, watching the sorcerer. Then she, too, begins speaking. She makes a small symbol of her own, and then her hands relax.

Grimpen snorts. "She cannot save us!" he rasps. "Neither her magic nor mine is strong enough! We must flee while we can!"

"I will not leave," Father Justin says slowly, shaking his head. "I will add my own power to help stop this evil man!"

"What's going to happen?" you gasp, frightened by the look on the wizard's face.

"A meteor swarm!" Grimpen hisses. "He'll cast four fireballs, one to each corner of the room, and they'll explode! The blast of one alone is enough to kill any creature in this room. Four will fry us like so many fish!"

Luben's voice rises steadily. He is obviously nearing the end of his spell. Grimpen Seventhson turns and starts to leave.

"We have only moments!" he warns.

"What if the Blue Lady isn't powerful enough to protect us?" your brother asks.

1) "I'm going to stay with the Blue Lady no matter what!" you declare. "She's counting on us!" If this is what you say, turn to page 79.

2) "I'm going to get out of here!" you cry. If this is what you decide, turn to page 10.

You haven't gone far when the corridor slants off in a new direction, heading east. The floor becomes smoother and the air warmer. You smell a faint, sweet scent in the air. The corridor comes to an abrupt end. Ahead, you see a small door, barely big enough for a person to crawl through. The door is made of wood and opens easily.

"There are no wererat tracks," Eric mutters.

"And I don't sense any evil here," Father Justin adds, shaking his head. "I feel a great goodness and sense of well-being. I believe we may go ahead in safety."

"You go first," you tell Eric.

"Good idea," he says. "I'm glad you're learning something."

He bends down, nearly stooping double to fit through the doorway. You follow, your knife in your hand, although you don't feel as if you are in any danger. The room you enter is dark and smells like . . .

"Flowers!" you exclaim in astonishment.

The wizard pokes his staff through the door and its light fills the room. You look around. The round room is filled from top to bottom with exotic flowering plants. At the far end of the room is a silver door, decorated with flowers carved in silver. You enter the room, marveling at the beautiful colors and wondering how they grow in such a dark place.

"Don't touch them," warns Father Justin unnecessarily. "They must be magic to grow in such a place."

Eric examines the door carefully, then calls, "Come have a look at this, Gregor. See if you can find some way to open it."

You study the door, thinking about everything Hugo taught you, but in the end you must admit defeat. There is no latch, no lock, no secret catch. You, Eric, and Bloodstone push at the door with all your might, and the wizard even tries a spell—all to no avail. The door remains closed. You stare at each other in frustration. Then an old story of Hugo's comes to mind. You stand back and run your eyes over the door's intricate design.

"That's it!" you cry. "Look, Eric!" With your forefinger, you trace a design on the door. It is exactly the shape and size of Lord Bloodstone's Sword of Valor.

"I see!" Your brother steps forward and holds the sword up to the door. Immediately the silver door absorbs the silver sword and swings open on silent hinges.

You are nearly blinded by a radiant blue light as a soft, deep voice calls, "Welcome to the Tomb of the Blue Lady."

Please turn to page 133.

"I don't trust you, Luben Warlock!" you declare. "Your ideas of happiness and mine probably aren't at all the same. The only way we'll have a happy ending is for you to be banished from this realm forever!"

The sorcerer's face twists into an ugly snarl. "Is this how you all feel?" he demands.

"Gregor speaks for all of us," Eric replies, smiling proudly at you.

"Then prepare to die!" Luben Warlock screams. He raises his hands, and suddenly he is no longer handsome. You feel terror overwhelm you as you stare at his hideously contorted features, and you turn away.

The Blue Lady puts her arm around your shoulder. "Do not be afraid, Gregor," she tells you gently. "What you see is his soul, the darkness that has consumed his very being. Face it, Gregor. Face the darkness! Only then can it be conquered!"

Taking a deep breath, you turn and stare directly at the evil wizard. At first you are so frightened that you want to run, but then you feel your brother's hand touch yours. You draw a deep breath, and your fear subsides.

The Blue Lady and Eric stand together, hand in hand. The Blue Lady has her other hand on your shoulder. You draw your brother close. Eric reaches out and grasps the wizard's gnarled and wrinkled hand.

Grimpen appears startled, then sighs. "I suppose I always knew it would come to this," he grumbles, leaning on Eric for support.

Father Justin addresses the evil wizard. "We have no need to fight you, Luben Warlock," the cleric states simply. "Our battles have all been fought, and we are victorious. The forces of good filling this room leave no room for you. Begone!"

"Begone, sorcerer!" Eric shouts, and you and the others join in.

Luben Warlock's face twists and writhes hideously. "Shrivel and die!" he screams. He raises his hand, shrieking out magic words—but nothing happens! He stares at you in astonishment.

"His evil is turning inward upon itself," the Blue Lady murmurs.

Even as you watch, you see the sorcerer begin to shrivel, his face wrinkled and twisted. "No!" he screams. "My power is insurmountable! This can't be happening!"

You watch in awe as the sorcerer shrinks smaller and smaller, then vanishes completely, leaving only a tiny spot on the floor.

The wizard's staff glows softly. The Silver Moon and Stars dim, then fade and die. You stand together, silent, feeling empty.

Suddenly Grimpen Seventhson snatches his hand away from Eric's and wipes it on his robe. "About time, too! Hand-holding, at my age! Humphf!" he snorts. You stare at the wrinkled wizard for a moment, then you see his eyes begin to sparkle. You begin to laugh, and soon everyone is laughing and the tension you've all felt for so long is broken.

"Is the curse gone?" you ask.

"We'll soon see," Father Justin says mysteriously, smiling. "What will you do now, Gregor?"

You don't even hesitate. You look up at your brother and smile broadly. "I want to come and live at Bloodstone Manor," you say. "If—if my brother will teach me how to become a nobleman."

"I'm afraid that's something your brother has to learn himself," Lord Bloodstone says with a sigh. He smiles back at you. "It won't be easy, Gregor. I've been living in a bottle for a long time. But with your help, we can fight my problem together."

"And what about you, Eric?" Father Justin asks. "What will you do now?"

Eric and the Blue Lady stand close together, surrounded by a radiant blue light. "We are going back to my kingdom to be married," he replies firmly. "There we will rule together, she as my strength and I as hers. Our love will become my sword and my shield."

"And you, Grimpen Seventhson?" Father Justin turns to the aged wizard.

Grimpen Seventhson scowls and shuffles his feet. "Well . . . if you must know," he grumbles, "I'm going to continue the good work of my master, Ian Whitestone. I will start with this wretched town, helping the people to begin their lives over again." He glares at all of you. "But if any of you dare mention that to a soul, I'll—I'll turn you all into toads!"

Grimpen winks at you, but you already knew his threat wasn't really serious. So, apparently, does Father Justin.

"Then I say the curse is ended!" Father Justin raises his amulet high overhead, at arm's length. A beam of pure white light pierces through the ceiling of the catacombs and strikes the amulet.

You watch in wonder as the chamber in which you stand begins to glow brightly in the white light, increasing steadily until you are forced to close your eyes.

When you open them once more, the catacombs have vanished. You find yourself standing instead in the hall of Bloodstone Manor. Outside, you hear bells ringing and people shouting merrily.

Looking out the window, you see trees blooming as if making up for years of lost springs. The sun is shining and the air is warm and fragrant, but you know that spring is only a fleeting season. Summer will come. The crops will flourish and grow. Autumn will bring harvest, and then winter will arrive, with its chill winds and killing frosts. And you know that this is all a part of life. But winter will not be dark, because there will always be the promise of spring.

THE END

ENDLESS QUEST® Books
From the producers of the
DUNGEONS & DRAGONS® Game

- #1 DUNGEON OF DREAD
- #2 MOUNTAIN OF MIRRORS
- #3 PILLARS OF PENTEGARN
- #4 RETURN TO BROOKMERE
- #5 REVOLT OF THE DWARVES
- #6 REVENGE OF THE RAINBOW DRAGON
- #7 HERO OF WASHINGTON SQUARE
- #8 VILLAINS OF VOLTURNUS
- #9 ROBBERS AND ROBOTS
- #10 CIRCUS OF FEAR
- #11 SPELL OF THE WINTER WIZARD
- #12 LIGHT ON QUESTS MOUNTAIN
- #13 DRAGON OF DOOM
- #14 RAID ON NIGHTMARE CASTLE
- #15 UNDER DRAGON'S WING
- #16 THE DRAGON'S RANSOM
- #17 CAPTIVE PLANET
- #18 KING'S QUEST

For a free catalog, write
TSR, Inc.
P.O. Box 756, Dept. EQB
Lake Geneva, WI 53147

TSR™